"You're afraid of something, Mrs. Wheeler. I can help you, if you let me."

"This is unbelievable." Kate's voice escalated with each syllable. "Of course I'm afraid. You've just arrested me."

"How did your husband die?" Brody asked.

She flinched. The anger drained from her eyes before her gaze shifted downward. "He was murdered," she answered at last, sounding forlorn and defenseless.

Her distress affected Brody. He didn't want to be affected. He wanted to stay detached, uninvolved. But his protective instincts reared up, refusing to be ignored. "By whom?"

"I don't know."

"And you're afraid you're next?" He hadn't meant his tone to sound harsh.

Though her peaches-and-cream complexion turned to chalk, she lifted her chin and sat up straighter. The staunch bravado may have returned, but she couldn't quite hide the anxiety in her eyes.

D0054715

Books by Terri Reed

Love Inspired Suspense

Strictly Confidential #21
Double Deception #41

Love Inspired

Love Comes Home #258
A Sheltering Love #302
A Sheltering Heart #362
A Time of Hope #370

TERRI REED

grew up in a small town nestled in the foothills of the Sierra Nevada. To entertain herself, she created stories in her head and when she put those stories to paper, her teachers in grade school, high school and college encouraged her imagination. Living in Italy as an exchange student whetted her appetite for travel, and modeling in New York, Chicago and San Francisco gave her a love for the big city, as well. She has also coached gymnastics and taught in a preschool. She enjoys walks on the beach, hikes in the mountains and exploring cities. From a young age she attended church, but it wasn't until her thirties that she really understood the meaning of a faith-filled life. Now living in Portland, Oregon, with her college-sweetheart husband, two wonderful children, a rambunctious Australian shepherd and a fat guinea pig, she feels blessed to be able to share her stories and her faith with the world. She loves to hear from readers at P.O. Box 19555, Portland, OR 97280.

Double Deception

Terri Reed

Steeple
Hill®

Published by Steeple Hill Books™

STEEPLE HILL BOOKS

Steeple
Hill®

ISBN-13: 978-0-373-44231-7
ISBN-10:   0-373-44231-9

DOUBLE DECEPTION

www.SteepleHill.com

Printed in U.S.A.

Be strong and courageous,
do not be afraid or tremble at them,
for the Lord your God is the one who goes with
you. He will not fail you or forsake you.

—*Deuteronomy* 31:6

To my husband, my hero. I love you always and forever.

ONE

Brody McClain hated storms.

The pounding rain and swirling wind off the Nantucket Sound were relentless, like the nightmares that had plagued him for five years.

Old anger resurfaced and burned in his gut.

With a shake of his head, he pushed the memories aside and focused his attention back on the small cottage. *Concentrate.*

Lightning streaked across the sky and reflected off the windowpanes of the dark house, making the dormer windows glow like large, luminous eyes.

Brody crouched behind the branches of an ancient rhododendron. The blood in his head thudded in tempo with the rapid beat of his heart. He gritted his teeth, forcing his breathing under control.

After a moment, his vision cleared and his eyes adjusted to the night. Drops of rain streamed down his back, plastering his cotton shirt to his skin. *Should have grabbed a jacket, McClain.*

From beyond the house, above the roar of the

churning surf crashing against the cape, a seagull's high-pitched squawk protested the downpour.

I'm with you, buddy.

Blinding lightning pierced the midnight sky. More rumbling thunder nipped at its heels. Brody narrowed his gaze, staring at the large multipaned window near the front door, waiting impatiently for another flash to confirm what he thought he'd just seen.

Finally the light came. In that second of stunning brilliance he saw the silhouette.

Someone *was* in the house.

His fingers tightened around the grip of his Glock. He'd drawn his sidearm as he'd approached the house, heeding the familiar, gentle nudging he'd learned to respect. Only once had he ignored that inner signal. That mistake had cost him everything.

But that was then. Now… Brody moved soundlessly along the wraparound porch toward the back door. He tried the knob. Locked.

He pulled out a ring of keys and skimmed his finger along the flat surface of each, searching for the correct raised letter. He found the key marked with a *K*. He slipped it into the lock and opened the door.

A noise beyond the storm outside caught Kate Wheeler's attention. Just scraps of sound really, like a hinge in need of oil. The noise went perfectly with the eerie shadows that played along the covered furniture, making the white sheets appear ghostly. Musty staleness mingled with the salty scent of the Atlantic Ocean permeated the air.

She shivered in the darkness, her imagination wreaking havoc on her nerves with thoughts of some unknown assassin stalking her.

Outside, the wind howled across the Nantucket Sound, a forlorn noise that echoed through the house.

Fighting to keep her anxiety from turning into panic, Kate leaned against the wall.

Lord, I'm really scared. I need Your courage.

She never should have come here tonight. She should have done the smart thing and waited for morning before coming to the house she hoped held answers to her husband's death. But patience wasn't one of her virtues.

Now she was stranded. The airport limousine service had disappeared long ago and the cell phone tucked in her purse was useless, the battery dead and the recharge cord forgotten at home. Given the circumstances of Paul's death, she should have been more cautious.

Ever since his funeral the previous month, she'd had the uneasy feeling someone was watching her.

The sensation followed her everywhere, the constant impression of eyes observing her every move, taking stock, waiting for the right moment to attack.

I told them you have it.

Paul's dire words rang in her head. If only she knew what "it" was.

Her condo in Los Angeles had been ransacked twice, which led her to believe that they—whoever *they* were—hadn't found the mysterious object. She hoped she'd find answers to her questions here in this small Massachusetts town, starting with this place—a house she'd known nothing about.

She glanced around as hurt burrowed in deep. How long had Paul owned this oceanfront cottage? Why had he bought a house when he'd refused to purchase one with her, his wife?

Once she would have expected the trappings of a normal marriage.

Paul's courtship had been the epitome of romance. They'd met at a Chamber of Commerce mixer. She'd been taken with his blond good looks and professional demeanor. He'd wooed her with candlelit dinners, roses at her door every Friday and touching love letters. She hadn't been able to resist his hard press. He'd represented stability and security: everything she longed for, everything that had been missing in her childhood.

But after the wedding, he'd changed. Even though he'd championed her career, urging her to advance rapidly through the ranks of the bank where she worked, he'd become distant at home. At first she'd attributed his withdrawal to difficulty adjusting to marriage.

As time wore on, she'd become more confused. She didn't know what she'd done to make him pull away. Throughout their four-year marriage, they'd been both physically and emotionally separated. The lack of love, respect and affection had cut her to her soul.

She'd tried everything to keep the marriage intact. She'd prayed every day. She'd sought professional help. But Paul had refused to go to counseling. He'd refused to talk to their pastor. He'd even stopped attending church. When people asked about him, she didn't know what to say. They'd become strangers living in the same apartment.

Now he was dead and she was left to clean up the mess.

She pushed away from the wall. Though she'd never been afraid of the dark, the lack of electricity in the little seaside bungalow unnerved her. She moved to the rustic side table and finally located matches and a candle in the bottom drawer.

With shaky hands, Kate struck the match. Nothing. On her second try the little stick sputtered to life with a small burst of flame and she held the fire against the candle's wick. But if she'd thought the light would quell her uneasy feeling, she was mistaken. Beyond the circle of light, the glow flickered, deepening the shadows and adding to the spooky feel of the room.

The wind increased in tempo. A branch grated along a wall and a chill darted over Kate's flesh, raising goose bumps along her skin. A gust of air blew through the living room and the candle's flame careened crazily out of control before sputtering to a silent death. Inky darkness once again descended, enveloping her.

Suddenly, the familiar sense of being watched became acute, wrapping around Kate like greedy hands, stealing her breath. She shuddered. She glanced about the room, the blackness overwhelming, menacing.

Nothing's there. No one had been there for a month. She was safe here. She had to be.

Moving quickly toward the entryway where she'd left her suitcases and purse, Kate decided to find a bedroom where she could curl up beneath the blankets and wait for morning. Answers would be found in the daylight.

A flash of lightning exploded and threw the ebony

night into stark relief. Her world appeared like a photo negative.

The harsh light illuminated the retreating figure of a man as he moved away from her through the kitchen.

A man with a gun.

The blood drained from her head. For a split second she wrestled with the sensation of dizziness. Her heart clutched before pounding in large, booming beats. The roar of blood rushing back to her brain flooded her ears, blocking out the sounds of the night.

He would see her if she moved to the front door. Her gaze darted in the direction of the bedrooms. If he found her there she'd be trapped. But what choice did she have? The bags slid from her slackened fingers to land soundlessly on the small area rug beneath her feet. *Please, Lord, protect me.* Because no one on earth would.

Then all was black again.

Once inside the cottage, Brody listened for any telltale sounds of the intruder, but the nocturnal noises beyond the walls of the house taunted his caution. Not wanting to announce his presence yet, he kept his flashlight attached to his belt.

Silently, he moved from the kitchen into the dining room. A large wooden table and several chairs made the area difficult to negotiate in the dark.

He breathed in. Beyond the musty, rank smell of disuse, an out-of-place scent drifted past his nostrils. The acrid smell of a burnt match.

On heightened alert, Brody moved forward, leading with his firearm. Once free of the dining room, he entered the living room. Another smell. A fragrance he recognized from his mother's garden—the sweet scent of lilacs.

Light flashed. A sharp, loud bang exploded into the stillness and ricocheted off the walls.

Brody dove for cover. His heart hammered in his chest. Adrenaline pumped through his veins and his nerves stretched taut. For a beat of time he was back in Boston, seeing the flare of gunfire, reliving the agony of betrayal.

The sounds of his own breath wiped the memory away. *Thunder, you idiot.* The storm was playing games with his mind.

Crawling to the wall, he pressed his throbbing hip and back against its cool surface. He took a deep, calming breath and focused on the one constant in his life, his job. He could never forget what he had to do.

Peering around the corner into the entryway, he caught sight of a dark shape. He froze, his heart picked up speed again. Though his vision was 20/20, the darkness made it difficult to see. Brody expelled a harsh breath. He had no choice. He had to get closer.

Lying prone and using his forearms to move his body forward, Brody crept across the threshold between the two rooms, over the cold hardwood floor toward the dark form. Three feet away, he released the breath he'd been holding.

Luggage. Black leather, two large and one small carry-on type. He frowned and moved closer. He nudged them. Full.

What was going on?

A fragment of noise came from down the hall, toward

the bedrooms. He slowly rose and in a low crouch, proceeded into the gloom of the long hallway. He stopped to listen for more sound to direct his way. None came.

He paused at the first door he came to and listened for a moment. No noise. Still he braced himself, fisted his flashlight and turned the knob. The door swung open. Brody flipped on the flashlight. His gaze swept the room. Nothing beneath the bed. But the closet…

Out of habit, he glanced over his shoulder, making sure no one was behind him. He pressed his back into the wall, closed his hand over the closet doorknob and slowly turned.

Kate had to find a way out of the house.

She stood in the middle of the second bedroom. A bed, a dresser, a nightstand and a closet. There was nowhere to hide. Forget the closet. She couldn't take being in the small, confining space. Better to face her enemy and die in the open than wait meekly in what very well could be her coffin.

Chills slid over her body.

She didn't dare go back down the hall, so that left the window above the bed. Stepping up onto the mattress, she grasped the handle and pulled upward.

The window wouldn't budge. She tried the lock, but it refused to give. Using all of her strength, she managed to turn the lock, and yet the window still wouldn't move. Running a hand over the wood, she found the problem. The window had been nailed shut.

She gritted her teeth in frustration as she fought desperate panic. The logical part of her mind that had always ruled her life clamped down on the urgent impulse to dive head-first through the glass and hope she got away in one piece.

An idea formed in her mind. Something she'd seen in a movie or read in a book.

Lord, let this work in real life.

Kate snatched the brass bedside lamp, yanking the cord from the wall. Taking a deep breath, she raised her arm and threw the lamp with all her might at the window. Glass shattered in a shower of chunks and slivers, mostly landing in the dirt on the outside the house, some falling inward onto the bed.

She cringed at the noise, then jumped from the bed and ran across the room to press her body against the wall beside the hinges of the door bare seconds before it burst open. The doorknob connected with her hipbone and she bit her lip to stifle a cry.

In hypnotic terror, she watched as the broad back of a man appeared within her line of vision. *Please, don't let him find me.*

She squeezed farther into the corner. The man stopped in front of the open closet door, his head cocked to one side. He moved out of her view and she heard the barely perceptible creak of the mattress and a powerful beam of light lit the room. Kate closed her eyes and prayed her ruse had worked and he thought she'd escaped.

The light went out and she heard a soft thud. He'd stepped off the bed. A second later she heard him move toward the doorway. Tensing, she waited.

Through the crack between the door and the jamb she saw him pass by, a dimmer shape against the darkness. Relief coursed through her, making her knees weak. She hadn't been found. *Thank You, Lord.*

Minutes ticked by. She heard the solid click of the front door being closed, the sound of the man retreating to take his search into the night. The waiting seemed eternal before she gathered enough nerve to emerge from behind the door.

Should she go through the house to escape? She turned to look at the broken window. The jagged edges would cut her to shreds. She didn't have any choice. She had to go through the house.

Brody stood poised with his back against the wall at the mouth of the long, dark hallway. Clever trick, breaking the glass to make it look as if his prey had jumped out the window and escaped.

The second Brody had entered the bedroom he'd known he wasn't alone. A tightening of his senses had made him aware of the other's presence.

Even if his instincts hadn't alerted him, he still would have known. No one could have gone out that window without cutting themselves and leaving a trail of blood. Besides, the lack of footprints in the soft, mossy dirt below the window, visible in his flashlight's beam, had been a dead giveaway.

So he waited. Waited as a honed patience calmed his heart and readied his body. It was only a matter of time.

Inch by inch, Kate made her way down the pitch-black corridor, her hand guiding her past the doors to the other rooms. As she neared the living room she stopped. A familiar, yet strange sensation tickled her spine. She wasn't alone.

On some deep, basic level she felt the man's presence, sensed his heartbeat. She pressed her back flat against the wall and balled her hands into tight fists. It wasn't fair. But then, God never promised life would be fair, only that He'd be there.

Her gaze slid from the grayer light of the house back to the darkness of the windowless hall. Was he behind her in the dark, inching his way toward her? Taking her lip between her teeth to keep tears and welling panic at bay, she stood immobile, unsure what her next move should be.

Tension coiled, her stomach churned and her lungs burned. She couldn't go back. She had to go forward.

With a deep breath, she pushed from the wall and forced her legs to move fast. Adrenaline coursed through her limbs and her heart raced. She could see the front door. She just had to make it across the open entryway. Three more feet…iron cords wrapped around her, stopping her momentum with a jerk. She screamed as she was tackled to the ground.

Her head smacked against the hardwood and spots of light exploded before her eyes. A huge, muscled body landed on top of her, effectively pinning her beneath his hulking figure, and drove the air from her lungs.

Fear blasted up her spine. She was going to die, and it was all Paul's fault.

With a grip of steel, the man yanked her arms over her head and held her wrists captive while another probing hand ran over her body. Numbing shock rippled through her, then the roaming hand stilled.

The man swore in a deep hiss near her ear and eased off her.

She took a shallow breath.

"You're a woman," a deep, rich voice accused.

The observation seemed ridiculous. Of course she was a woman. Did Paul's murderer think Paul had been married to a monkey?

The ridiculous thought brought fear raging headlong into her consciousness. This man was here to get something she hadn't a clue about, and then he would probably kill her the way he'd killed Paul. Then another thought flittered across her mind: what if he assaulted her before killing her? *Oh, Lord, take me home quickly.*

No. Not yet. Sheer terror spurred her into action. She twisted and turned, her body bucking in an effort to throw him off balance. Her hands pulled against the restraint of his grip, her legs struggled to find leverage on the floor, pushing and kicking wildly. The toe of her shoe made contact with a shin, eliciting a grunt of pain from her attacker. A moment of satisfaction brought a tightening to her lips.

Her knee flew upward but he rolled slightly, deflecting her hit to his hip. She ground her back teeth. She wasn't going to let him win. She wasn't ready to die.

"Hey, lady. Calm down."

Calm down? He wanted her calm so he could kill her. Her grandmother had taught her that God hadn't made women to be passive, but proactive. She'd fight with everything she had before she'd calmly let this man do her in.

Arching upward, she used her forehead as a ramming device. She connected with his chin, causing his teeth to come together with a snap. Pain shot through her.

For a moment his grip lessened and she took advantage of the opportunity. Freeing a hand, she lashed out, aiming for his eyes. She fell short, her nails raking sharply down his face, evoking a yowl of pain.

"That's it!" The harsh words echoed through the house. He held her hands in a grip so tight she knew she'd never get free.

"*No!*" But still she fought, determined not to give up until the last breath left her body. Too many questions remained unanswered, too much pain still lived in her heart. Blind fear made her body convulse, desperate to break free.

The chink of metal somewhere above her head made her close her eyes. She didn't want to see the torture device he would use on her and she prayed for oblivion. Oblivion and a painless death.

She cried out in surprise as he twisted her arm behind her and flipped her over. Cold metal encircled her wrists. A sharp snap filled her ears. And only then, from the far reaches of sanity, did she realize she'd been handcuffed. The man spoke in low, smooth tones, but her terror-fogged mind couldn't grasp the words.

"Do you understand?" The steady cadence of his words, the richness of his voice, washed over her and a sense of unreality set in. Closing her eyes tightly, she readied herself for the journey to heaven.

The man grasped her shoulders and gently shook her. "Do you understand? Answer me!"

"No." She didn't understand why she was about to die. She didn't understand how she'd come to this point in time. And she didn't understand how she could have been so wrong about Paul. Who had she been married to? What kind of man had he really been? And why had he allowed this to happen to her? Unfortunately, she would die without the answers.

"Lady, how hard is it to understand? You're under arrest."

TWO

The woman beneath him stilled.

"Arrest?" The word came out in a dry croak.

"Yes, you're under arrest." Brody couldn't see her face but he heard the rapid labor of her breath, felt the rise and fall of her chest where their ribs connected. And he was all too aware of the fact that his intruder was female. Soft and full of curves. The smell of lilacs he'd detected earlier wasn't a remnant of the owner's last visit, sporadic as they were.

The scent clung to his captive's hair.

Pushing away, he came to his knees and helped her to a sitting position.

"You're...you're not here...to kill me?" Her voice faded to a hushed stillness and Brody heard the fear behind the words.

"I'm not going to kill you," he said in a calming tone. "Do you understand that anything you say can be used against you in a court of law—"

She made an odd noise. "You're a cop?"

"Yes, ma'am. You have the right to an attorney. If—"

"I haven't done anything," she interrupted.

Brody ignored her protest and finished her Miranda rights then helped her to her feet as a bolt of lightning whitewashed the room. He caught a glimpse of an impish face and large, luminous eyes. The tip of her head barely reached the top of his shoulder. So much -spirit in one so little. A spark of admiration for the way she'd fought him flared hot.

The light faded and the shadows returned, leaving him feeling unsettled. She certainly didn't look like a criminal.

He heard her test the strength of the metal links between the cuffs.

"Are these really necessary?"

In the blackness, her voice rang cool and clear, yet Brody heard the underlying tension in her tone. Why did she think someone was out to kill her?

"I'll take them off when we get to the station." His natural caution took precedence. Regardless of the gender of his intruder, experience had taught him how deceptive people could be—especially the female sort.

"The police station?"

"Actually, the county sheriff's office. Let's go." His terse answer harbored no room for discussion.

"My purse!"

Brody paused by the grouping of luggage. He picked up the leather bag that he'd mistaken for a carry-on piece of luggage. "This?"

She nodded.

The damp shirt on his back itched and the house grew colder by the minute, making his hip hurt and his limbs grow numb. He resisted the urge to limp by placing a hand on her arm to guide her out of the house. She tried to pull away but he tightened his hold.

Beneath his palm, she trembled as he helped her into his cruiser. Her flowery, lilac scent once again reminded him of his mother's garden. A place where he used to find a sense of serenity. Even if he took up Mom's constant invitations to come home, he doubted he'd find that kind of peace now.

With the heater cranked high, they rode in silence through the small town of Havensport, Massachusetts, the quaint buildings of the New England community surveyed by Brody with a sheriff's eye.

Stores dark and locked tight, no suspicious characters roaming the streets. There never were. Until tonight. Havensport was as boringly safe as a small town could get, but old habits were hard to break.

The sheriff's office kept keys of all the summer homes in case of emergencies. Lucky for Pete Kinsey that Mae Couch, the elderly lady who lived next door, had been looking out her window and seen someone lurking about. So unusual an occurrence was it, Sheriff Brody McClain had immediately responded.

He glanced in the rearview mirror. The woman's face was turned toward the window, but he could make out the straight line of her nose, which tilted upward slightly at the tip and a wide, generous mouth set into a firm crease. She hadn't spoken since they'd left the house.

Within the enclosed space of his cruiser he couldn't tell the color of her hair. The lights of the station would tell him soon enough. He returned his gaze forward as he slowed to park the car in his spot by the door of the station.

The Havensport County Sheriff's Office stood at one end of town like a sentinel on guard duty. Though the redbrick building, built in the early part of the century with a high peaked roof and multipaned windows, had withstood updates both in and out, it still remained a historical landmark, due mainly to the fact that the first sheriff's family still owned most of the property within a thirty-mile radius around the town.

Brody got out and opened the back door. The woman refused his help and struggled out of the vehicle on her own. With reluctance, he again felt admiration for her grit.

Rain poured from the sky, rolling in rivulets down his face. Quickly, he ushered his charge into the station.

Her hair was copper. He'd always liked redheads. He should have stuck with them instead of being tempted by Elise's willowy blond good looks.

The station's warmth seeped through his drenched clothing, bringing life back to his numb limbs and chasing away the cold reality of Elise.

After settling the woman into a chair, he unlocked the handcuffs. She rubbed at the rough, red marks left by the metal rings. Brody lowered his gaze and busied himself at the antique oak desk, ignoring the uncomfortable twinge of guilt that rose at the sight of her reddened, slender wrists.

Deputy Warren Teal stepped from the bathroom, still drying his hands with a paper towel. "Hi, boss."

Warren's curious gaze settled on Kate as he crumpled the sheet into a ball. After tossing it into the wastebasket, he perched his lean frame on the edge of Brody's desk. "What do we have here? This the perp at the Kinsey house?"

Brody arched a brow at the deputy. The young rookie was overeager at times, but fairly competent.

"Sorry." Warren moved away and sat at the only other desk in the room. "She do that to your face?"

Ignoring the questions and the reminder of his stinging cheek, Brody took a blank report, a pen—he preferred to write out the reports first and key them in later—then turned to the woman. "Name?"

Her gaze pinned him to his chair. Confusion radiated from the depths of her large green eyes. "You don't know?"

Brody's mouth twisted with wry amusement. "Lady, I'm good, but not that good."

She blinked. "Why did you arrest me?"

"B and E is a felony, ma'am." At her blank expression, he clarified, "Breaking and entering."

"I didn't break in," she insisted, leaning forward. "I own the house. My late husband left the property to me." Her voice wavered. "If you'll let me call my attorney, he'll be able to straighten this whole mess out."

He glanced at her left hand. No band of gold encircled her ring finger. "Pete Kinsey's your husband?" That was a surprise. The womanizing stockbroker had commented often enough how marriage turned men into jellyfish. Not exactly the marrying type.

"My husband's name was Paul Wheeler. He owned the house. Pete Kinsey was my husband's business partner."

Warren turned in his chair, his gray eyes round with interest. "Pete never mentioned a business partner." He shook his head in bemusement. "Wow, can that man party."

Pete Kinsey's parties were legendary on the Cape. Every summer he'd host a big bash with the big society types in attendance—Hollywood celebrities, corporate big shots, political figures. The affair lasted a full weekend and the locals looked forward to the money it brought in. And as long as they didn't break any laws, Brody left them alone.

"Don't you have some work to do, Warren?"

The deputy shrugged and picked up a report.

Intrigued by the situation and by the petite redhead, Brody tapped his pen against the form in front of him as he studied her. "Your full name?"

"Katherine Amanda Wheeler."

Brody wrote out her name. "Address?"

The Beverly Hills address took him by surprise. "You're a long way from home."

She ignored his comment. "Don't I get a phone call?"

"As soon as I have the paperwork filled out." He laid his hand on her purse which he'd deposited on top of his desk. "Is your ID in here?"

"Yes."

He picked up the satchel and unzipped it. "Mind?"

Her deprecating gaze bored into him. "Do I have a choice?"

"No." But still he waited for permission.

"Then go ahead."

He dumped the contents of her purse onto the desktop. A compact, a black tube of lipstick, three granola bars and a thick black wallet spilled out. He unclasped the single snap on the folded wallet and plucked her ID from the first plastic sheath. He wrote down the information on the form. "Your occupation?"

"I work for Valley Savings Bank as the Vice President of Operations. You want to call my boss for a reference?"

Brody cocked his brow. "No. That won't be necessary."

She rolled her eyes. The harsh fluorescent light overhead failed to wash out the sparks of fire in her shoulder-length hair. His gaze strayed to the curling ends where they teased the collar of her pink silk blouse. He tightened his grip on the pen in his hand to keep from reaching out to test the curls. Would they be as silky as they looked?

Her clothing spoke of the kind of money that went along with her address. The tailored suit she wore, though wrinkled and damp, couldn't hide the curves beneath.

"What were you doing there, Mrs. Wheeler?" he questioned, bringing his mind back to business.

"I wanted to see the house." Katherine wrapped her arms around herself. He noticed her shiver while some of the fight drained from her eyes. The coat he'd failed to take with him hung on the back of his chair. Reaching behind him, he grabbed the jacket and handed it to her.

She wrapped the too-large jacket around her shoulders. "Thanks."

He gave a short nod of his head. She looked small

and vulnerable and in need of protection. Seeing her in his coat made his chest burn. Irritably, he pushed the phone across the desk. "Make your call."

He didn't have to offer twice. Her long, tapered fingers moved over the keypad. Brody watched her hands and then, like a gawker at a crime scene, his gaze was drawn to her mouth. Pink, soft-looking. Well-shaped lips. Kissable lips

Yanking his mind away from that treacherous path, he decided he was more tired than he'd thought. The last thing he should be thinking about was his suspect's kissability.

He forced his attention back to the phone, on the faint metallic sound of a male voice coming through the line. From the look of consternation on Katherine's face, he guessed an answering machine had picked up.

"Gordon, its Kate. You won't believe this. I'm at the Havensport Sheriff's office, of all things. The number here is..." She raised her brows in question.

Brody gave her the number, which she repeated into the phone before hanging up. Circles of fatigue darkened the skin beneath her eyes, and he shifted uncomfortably in his chair. He dearly wished his mother hadn't raised a gentleman. Despite how much he might want to let Katherine Wheeler go lie down, he still had questions that needed answers.

Swallowing his inclinations, he got back to business. "Why did you think someone was coming to the house to kill you?"

A watchful wariness filled her gaze. "I was alone. You attacked me. What was I supposed to think? That you wanted to dance?"

A spurt of amusement kicked up the corner of Brody's mouth.

She picked up his nameplate and toyed with it between her slender hands. Her manicured nails clicked against the brass. "Where do we go from here?"

"I need to verify your story, check out your ID—"

"And then?" She lifted an auburn brow.

"Then you'll tell me what kind of trouble you're in."

For a brief second her gem-colored gaze locked with his before darting away. "The only trouble I have is you, Sheriff."

Brody smiled grimly, tossed his pen on the desk and sat back in his chair. *Here we go again.*

She was lying.

On the mean streets of Boston, Brody had learned how to read people, learned to watch for the signs, and she definitely showed signs. And this time he wasn't going to ignore the obvious. She was holding back and not for one second did he believe she'd thought him a random intruder.

The scratches left by her nails itched, reminding him of her blind terror. He dabbed at his face with a tissue. Tiny spots of red soaked into the material. "So, what has you so spooked?"

"Are you going to book me, Sheriff McClain?" Her knuckles turned white around the nameplate. "I'm cold and tired. And I don't want to sit here while you play amateur psychologist."

He would have been amused if he hadn't noticed the fleeting look of disdain in her eyes. She didn't know the extent of how much psychobabble he could recite or the reasons why. He told himself to forget it, not to offer his help or advice. "You're afraid of something, Mrs. Wheeler. I can help you, if you let me."

"This is unbelievable." Her voice escalated with each syllable. "Of course I'm afraid. You've just arrested me." Her eyes flared with anger, deepening in color to a dark forest green.

"How did your husband die?"

She flinched. The anger drained from her eyes before her gaze shifted downward and her fingers flexed around his nameplate.

"He was murdered," she answered at last, sounding forlorn and defenseless.

Her distress affected him. He didn't want to be affected. He wanted to stay detached, uninvolved. But his protective instincts reared up, refusing to be ignored.

"By whom? Do you think Pete Kinsey killed him?"

"I don't know."

"And you're afraid you're next?" He hadn't meant for his tone to sound harsh.

Though her peaches-and-cream complexion turned to chalk, her chin lifted and she sat up straighter. The staunch bravado may have returned, but she couldn't quite hide the anxiety in her eyes.

"So what happens now?" she questioned.

Brody tore his gaze from the slight cleft dimpling the middle of her chin. "You're my guest until I can verify your story, because as far as I know, Pete Kinsey owns that house." He stood and motioned her toward the cell. The small, barred cubicle was barren except for a cot, a pillow and a blanket.

"You've got to be kidding!"

"It's not the presidential suite, but it's better than most, and it's clean." And safe.

Those bright green eyes glared at him with haughty indignation that rivaled his younger sister Meghan's. He smothered a smile.

Kate moved into the cell and turned her back on him. An unsettling protest nagged at Brody. He didn't like seeing the petite redhead behind bars. She seemed harmless and innocent, hardly a hardened criminal.

He took a step and pain shot down his leg, reminding him sharply that appearances could be deceiving. He'd learned his lesson and he'd sworn never again to let a pretty face distract him from his job. He shifted his weight and eased the pain.

"Here." Kate slipped the jacket from around her shoulders and shoved it at him. He took it, then closed the cell door, along with the door to his bleeding heart.

Exhaustion overtook Kate and seeped into her bones, making her limbs heavy with lassitude. She grabbed the blanket from the cot and fluffed the pillow with her fist.

Sleeping in a jail cell wasn't exactly how she'd planned on spending her first night on the east coast, especially not on charges of breaking and entering.

She'd probably said more than she should. Her lawyer had sternly told her not to say anything, ever, without his presence. A self-deprecating grimace pulled at her mouth. Of course, if she'd heeded Gordon's advice and not left town, she wouldn't be incarcerated right now.

Sitting down on the narrow, makeshift bed, she muttered, "Better a jail cell than a coffin."

Her hands twisted the rough blanket. The material grew warm beneath her palms. Her lips formed a wry smile. *Thank You, Lord, for giving me such a safe place to sleep tonight.*

She looked at the sheriff. From a distance, his big, male body wasn't nearly as intimidating while hunched in front of his computer screen, his large fingers stabbing at the keys.

The set of his square jaw revealed his concentration and she doubted he realized his dark, wavy hair still glistened with rainwater. His soaked brown uniform emphasized his wide shoulders and broad chest. She could appreciate his masculine appeal with him across the room, but with him up close she'd found herself struggling to breathe evenly.

Abruptly, she shook off the notion of attraction and attributed the thudding of her heart to fear. A tight knot formed in her stomach. Soon, he would learn the complete story of Paul's death and the police's interest in her.

The sheriff had been too perceptive by half, his dark, intense eyes assessing her like an oddity. His questions and offer of help spoken in that much-too-pleasing accent had nearly unhinged her, making her want to open up, to tell him what haunted her nightmares. But Paul's final words echoed inside her head.

Trust...no one.

During the last several weeks, Kate's natural inclination to look for the good had dimmed until she was afraid even to allow herself to trust a man who should be trustworthy. But the police in Los Angeles had made her very aware that trust had to be earned.

The only person she remotely trusted now was Gordon Thomas, her lawyer. The kindly older gentleman had entered her life when her mother had hired him to deal with her divorce. Over the years he'd stayed a part of their lives, becoming a surrogate uncle for Kate, always willing to listen when she couldn't deal with her mother. Kate was grateful he'd taken an interest. Gordon had guided Kate in her college and career choices. She hated to think what path she'd have followed without his tutorship.

But this situation demanded she act on her own. She couldn't ever have the peace and security she craved if she didn't pursue the truth.

Her gaze wandered back to the sheriff. His dark hair fell across his forehead as he shifted in his seat, obstructing her view of his eyes, though she could see the angry red marks running down the side of his cheek left by her nails. She hoped he wouldn't scar, although she doubted even the puckering of wounded flesh could decrease the handsomeness of his ruggedly sculpted face.

Overhead, the lights dimmed and then blinked off and on. The sheriff lifted his head and their gazes locked. For a moment they stared at each other and a shaft of embarrassment darted up Kate's spine to settle in her cheeks. She was staring. She turned sharply away from his hooded, watchful eyes.

"Oh, man."

The sheriff's disgruntled voice brought her head back around.

"What's up?" Warren asked, his wiry form unfolding from his desk chair.

"Computer's down." The sheriff straightened and rolled his massive shoulders.

"You look done in. Why don't you head home? I'll stay here with the prisoner."

Kate stiffened at the deputy's words. Staring hard at the sheriff, she held her breath, waiting for his reply. Don't go. *Lord, please don't let him leave.*

Sheriff McClain leaned back in his chair and laced his fingers behind his head. His lids dropped, hiding the darkness of his eyes. After a heartbeat he replied, "No, I'll stay. But there's no sense in us both being here. You go on home to your pretty wife."

The deputy slanted Kate one last curious look, shrugged and picked up his jacket from the back of his chair. "Suit yourself. See you in the morning."

Kate breathed a sigh of relief as the deputy disappeared through the station door. While probably capable, the deputy just didn't seem as made for the task of protecting her as the sheriff did.

Her attention shifted back to Sheriff McClain. Didn't he have a wife to go home to? A wife waiting, worrying and wondering if he'd return or would this be the day he died for his dedication to his job? What type of woman would claim the love of a man with a dangerous occupation?

A woman like her own mother.

A woman unlike herself.

She squashed her curiosity. The sheriff's private life was none of her business. If he left his wife alone and lonely while he gave his job the attention his wife craved, what was that to her? Right now Kate needed him to do his job. She was thankful he'd stayed, but she wasn't going to dwell on the sheriff or why his presence was comforting.

Instead, she lay down on the cot and pulled the blanket to her chin. She doubted sleep would come, but closing her eyes and pretending sure beat staring at the too-handsome man who'd arrested her.

The storm's wrath didn't seem to penetrate the station walls and the room fell silent. Feeling relatively safe for the time being, Kate tried to relax. Unaccountably, she felt the sheriff would keep her from harm. God had put her in his care. She'd face her worries again with the new day.

Her body grew heavy and her lids felt weighted down as sleep settled in. Faintly, she heard a rustling of noise. The sheriff finally moving from his reclined position. His quiet footfalls echoed inside her head, but she was too groggy to open her eyes to see what he was doing.

Even when she heard the quiet click, then the slight squeak of the cell door opening, she couldn't muster up enough panic to rouse her from slumber.

She felt the added weight of another blanket being laid across her. With a sigh, she snuggled beneath the cocoon of rough material and drifted completely to sleep.

Brody stared at the sleeping woman.

Katherine Wheeler. No, he much preferred the informal Kate that she'd referred to herself as.

Why did he care if she grew cold? It shouldn't matter. But it did.

There was something compelling about her, something that pulled at him. Maybe it was the vulnerability he saw in her large, springtime eyes or the fact that she'd felt safe enough to allow herself to rest. Whatever the case, it had to stop. He couldn't allow himself to be drawn in by her.

Until Kate's story checked out, he had to think of her as a criminal. He half hoped she did own the house; he'd hate to see her end up in Walpole. Massachusetts Criminal Institute Cedar Junction was no place for such a pretty woman.

But then again, if what she said was true…what if she decided to become a resident of Havensport? Brody had an uneasy feeling that having her in the same town for any length of time would be hazardous to his carefully tended solitude.

Ha! As if you'd ever let a woman get close to you again, reprimanded his inner voice. *As if this woman, who drips with class, would ever want to get close to you.*

Brody drew back from the sleeping woman on the cot. He rubbed the spot on his hip where he bore the constant reminder of what trusting a woman could do. Old anger and helpless rage roared to life and Brody let out a compressed breath. He spun away and stalked back to his desk to stare at the blank computer screen.

The quicker he cleared up the mess with his guest, the better. Then his nice quiet life could resume the way he wanted it.

Alone.

THREE

Sunshine streamed through the barred window of the jail cell, spilling slanted lines of light across the cement floor and onto the cot where Kate lay. The warmth of the golden rays touched her cheek, and roused her from sleep.

Turning her head fully into the light, Kate frowned at the faint scent that clung to the air. She couldn't place it, but she knew it. A masculine fragrance, which stirred up images of a hard body pressed against her, a handsome face and a tender gesture.

The sheriff.

Kate's lids popped opened, her body tensed on the hard cot. Now she remembered where she was and why. Staring up at the gray ceiling of the jail cell, she listened for movement. Only the sounds of her own breathing met her ears. Was she alone in the jailhouse? She only had to turn her head to see through the black bars, but she stayed motionless, assessing her situation.

Strangely, she hadn't dreamed last night. One would think being locked up in a cold jail cell would bring her nightmares on full force. But she felt rested and ready to tackle the task of discovering why Paul had been murdered.

First she had to deal with Sheriff McClain.

Once Gordon explained about the house, the sheriff would have to let her go. But she had a disquieting feeling her association with the man wouldn't end there. He seemed the type to press, to find challenge in uncovering secrets. Her heart skipped a beat. Maybe the sheriff could help.

She sat up abruptly.

No. She couldn't trust anyone, save God. Even this man who'd sounded so sincere when he'd offered his help, who had cared enough to supply another blanket, who'd…she glanced down.

On the floor, next to her feet, sat a tray with juice, cereal and milk. Surprise and a good dose of pleased warmth suffused her.

Her gaze sought out the sheriff. He sat leaning over his desk with his cheek resting on his forearms. Asleep. He looked boyish, with waves of ebony spilling over his forehead and dark lashes splayed across his cheeks. Kate shook her head in wonder. Just when had Sheriff McClain brought the tray in? She'd heard the squeak of the cell door only once, when he'd brought her the blanket.

A violent shudder swept her body. She'd spent a dreamless night within the cell, lulled to sleep by a false sense of security. Anyone could easily have killed her in her sleep. *Anyone* being the sheriff.

But he hadn't.

Sheriff McClain was not the enemy. He hadn't known Paul. The man was simply a small-town sheriff doing his job. In her heart, she acknowledged that as truth, but her brain wasn't so sure.

Trust no one.

"Get a grip, girl," she muttered as she opened the milk carton and poured the liquid into the bowl of corn flakes. Paul's warning couldn't have extended to the sheriff. There was no reason she couldn't trust Brody McClain.

As she finished the cereal and was about to open the orange juice, a pained grunt split the air. Kate's gaze jumped to the sheriff. His once-relaxed features pulled back into a grimace, his head jerked and a moan slipped from between his lips.

She realized he was gripped within a nightmare. She knew what it was like to feel helplessly lost in the dark swirl of fear, memory and sleep. Compassion filled her chest until it ached with the need to relieve him of his dreams.

"Sheriff McClain?" Her voice bounced off the walls but held no power. "Sheriff?" she tried again, but to no avail. His head thrashed across his bent arms, his big body tense.

Taking a deep breath, Kate used her diaphragm to add more strength to her voice. "McClain!"

Her voice snapped through the station like the slam of a door.

As a wake-up call, it worked well.

Brody jerked his head up and blinked several times before he realized he was at the station, not on a darkened street in the middle of a storm facing the barrel of a gun.

His gaze met that of the woman occupying the cell.

Red curls framed her face, emphasizing her large, compassion-filled eyes. She'd witnessed his nightmare. *Great.*

Taking a shuddering breath, Brody composed himself and rose from his chair. Rigid, stiff muscles objected to the stretching. His limbs ached. The need to work out the kinks demanded his attention, but Brody had a job to finish first. The gym would have to wait.

He moved away from the desk to the coffee machine. With each step of his right leg, pain shot into his hip. He refused to allow himself the luxury of limping when meadow-green eyes followed his every move.

By rote, he went through the process of making strong coffee. Soon, the sound and smell of brewing French roast filled the air. Brody inhaled the rich scent for a moment, and pushed away the unease of Kate having witnessed what he worked so hard to keep beneath his heel. He walked steadily to the cell and opened the door. "Good morning."

His charge stared at him. Her head listed to the side and questions fairly radiated from her expression. "Good morning."

The corners of her mouth kicked up in a tentative smile that sneaked inside his chest and made it difficult to breathe.

"Thank you for breakfast…and the blanket."

He swallowed against both her gratitude and the effects of her smile. He didn't want either one. "I hope you slept well."

"I did, actually." She stood and stepped past him,

then stopped in the center of the room. She looked around uncertainly. "Is there a restroom I could use?"

"Down the corridor, on the left." Brody watched her disappear before he shifted his feet and took his weight onto his left leg, easing the ache in his right hip. Why was he bothering? It didn't make sense; vanity wasn't usually one of his faults. But letting her witness his weakness was…out of the question. He didn't want her to look at him with pity.

Most everyone in town knew vague details of how he'd acquired his limp. Few dared approach the subject and even fewer knew the truth of the situation. Taking a bullet was a hazard of the job that every law-enforcement officer faced. Only for Brody it was so much more and so much worse.

Forcing his torturous thoughts to recede, Brody limped over to his desk, sat down and tried to boot up the computer. The screen remained blank. He made a mental note to call the local computer expert and have him take a look at the infernal machine, which was always on the fritz. Somewhat ruefully, he figured he'd have to check out his guest the old-fashioned way.

As he reached for the phone, it rang, the shrill sound ringing hollow in the small station. Picking up the receiver, he answered, "Havensport County Sheriff's Office, Sheriff McClain speaking."

"I understand you have Katherine Wheeler in your custody." The gravelly voice boomed in Brody's ear, the tone sharp, the words clipped.

"And you are?"

"Gordon Thomas, Katherine's attorney."

Figured a Beverly Hills address could buy attitude. "She was caught breaking into one of our residents' summer home."

"The Kinsey residence?"

"Yes."

"The house belongs to my client."

Brody didn't like the condescending tone in the man's voice. "I'll need proof of that."

"What's your fax number?" the man asked curtly.

Brody rattled off the number and a few seconds later the machine in the corner beeped and hissed. Paper rolled out; sheet after sheet until finally it gave one final beep and remained silent.

"Sheriff McClain, I'd like to speak with Ms. Wheeler."

"Sorry, she's indispos…" Brody's voice trailed off as he noticed Kate standing beside his desk. Even with her wrinkled clothes and finger-combed hair, she radiated a quiet confidence. He'd give the lady credit; she was no fragile flower.

"Here she is."

Kate took the phone and turned away. He could hear the urgent note in the low tones of her voice. Picking up the fax, he flipped through the pages and realized Katherine Wheeler, though he liked *Kate* better, had been telling the truth. She now owned the house.

"Here, he wants to talk with you."

Kate's little smile grated on Brody's nerves. So she hadn't been lying. *Big whoop.* The fact that one female had the ability to tell the truth should make him happy, but he couldn't stop the unsettled feeling that something wasn't right. How did Pete Kinsey fit into this?

"Everything seems to be in order. I still have questions."

"I'm sure you do, Sheriff, but first things first. Release Mrs. Wheeler. There's no need for her still to be in your custody."

Brody wasn't so sure about that. He couldn't deny Kate's name appeared on the copies of her late husband's will and the deed to the house. She had every right to walk freely away and go about her life, yet he hesitated.

Mentally, he reviewed what he knew: Kate Wheeler's husband had been murdered, she'd inherited the Kinsey home. According to the paper faxed to him by the lawyer, the L.A.P.D. was investigating Paul's death but had yet to produce a suspect. All in all, the lawyer had supplied Brody with more information than required.

Legally, Brody had no reason to hold Kate, but it didn't sit well just to let her walk out. His protective impulses demanded he take her back to the house himself. For crying out loud, the woman had been terrified that someone was out to kill her, too.

Brody glanced at the blank computer and fervently wished the contraption hadn't gone on the blink. He would have liked to gather a bit more unbiased information.

Into the phone, Brody said crisply, "Mrs. Wheeler is free to go. I assume I can count on you to answer further questions?"

"Of course, Sheriff. Always happy to cooperate with the authorities."

The veiled sarcasm in Thomas's voice rang clear. Brody's hand tightened on the receiver. "I'll be in touch."

As soon as he'd put the receiver back in the cradle, Kate piped up. "I told you I owned the place. You should have given me the benefit of the doubt."

He slanted her a sideways glance. "Just doing my job, Mrs. Wheeler."

"I thought people were considered innocent until proven guilty?"

"Not in any reality I know." Brody's mouth quirked with a self-effacing grimace.

He'd been young and idealistic enough once to believe in the system, to believe that good triumphed over evil, that right always won out in the end, and that justice for all wasn't selective. But it was and he'd spent his adult life dedicated to making sure the innocent received their justice.

"But that's how it's supposed to work."

"*Supposed to* being the operative phrase."

Emotions flickered across Kate's face—anger and a touch of sadness. The impulse to take her into his arms and hold her until only joy reflected in the depths of her green eyes rose up sharply. He clenched his jaw. Been down that road. Not going again.

She shook her head. "This isn't the way God planned it, you know."

Her words poked at an old wound. He raised a brow. "What makes you think God gives a rip?"

Little creases appeared between her brows. "Because the alternative is unthinkable. Without God, there's no hope. Without hope, what's the point?"

"The point is to make it through each day." Refusing to let slip any of the betrayal he felt, he kept his voice neutral. "And if you live to see another day, you make it through that one."

"That's not living."

He shrugged. "It's surviving."

"That's missing out on all that God has to offer."

Her earnest expression tugged at him, but he could never forget or forgive. "Yeah, like heartache and pain. No, thanks."

"Who hurt you, Sheriff?"

The sincerity in her quietly asked question hit him in the chest like the business end of a nightstick. No way was he going to open up to her. No way was he going to allow anyone close again.

"I've seen more than my share of heartache and pain."

Compassion and skepticism warred in her eyes. Tension coiled in his veins. The moment she decided to let it go he released a concentrated breath.

Amusement entered her gaze. "Havensport doesn't exactly seem like crime central."

"Normally, it's not. You're the most excitement this town has seen in a while."

An auburn brow arched. "Oh, really."

Heat crept up his neck. *Real smooth, boyo.*

She was exciting in a dangerous way that had nothing to do with the law and everything to do with attraction. Not a good thing.

He cleared his throat. "I meant the breaking and entering."

Kate smiled and his gaze snagged on the cute little dimple in the middle of her chin. What would she do if he kissed her there?

His expression must have given away his thoughts because her smile faltered and a blush deepened the contours of her cheeks. She didn't look away.

"I'm sorry I scratched you."

Back to business, McClain. Forget about kisses. Kisses only led to betrayal.

"Are you ready to tell me what had you so scared?"

She lifted her delectable chin. "May I leave now?"

She was a tough little cookie. He liked that. "Come on, I'll take you back."

"I'll walk, thanks," she replied and headed for the door.

"I'll drive you."

With her hand on the doorknob, she glanced over her shoulder. "It's not that far."

"Doesn't matter, I'm taking you back."

With her hands on her hips, she glared at him. "I'm perfectly capable of seeing myself to my house."

She was beautiful with her face framed by red curls and those green eyes sparking with fire. He had no intention of getting burned no matter how beguiling the flame.

"Are you always this stubborn?"

"You're the one being stubborn," she declared with a huff.

She reminded him of a rookie cop with a chip on her shoulder. "Humor me, okay? Let me do my job and take you back to your house."

She regarded him steadily for a moment. "All right, fine. Do your job." She opened the door and walked out.

Brody picked up a fax data form and wrote out a request for information on the investigation of Paul Wheeler's murder. He dialed in the number for the

L.A.P.D. and sent the fax. He turned to go and his gaze landed on Kate's purse sitting on the floor next to his desk.

Her wallet still rested on the desktop. He picked it up. Maybe it was curiosity, maybe instinct, but instead of returning the wallet to the purse, he flipped it open. Plastic sheaths of photos, including her ID, separated the two halves. One side was lined with credit cards, gold and platinum. The other side held her checkbook.

He thumbed through the photos, a knot forming in his chest as his mind registered what he saw. There was a picture of Kate in a white wedding dress standing beside a tall, blond man. There was a photo of an older woman who he guessed to be her mother. Another picture of an older man in military uniform. Another less formal picture of the blond man. Brody slipped the picture out of the plastic. On the back, someone, Kate he presumed, had written the name Paul and the date of when the photo had been taken.

Brody tucked the picture into his shirt pocket. One question had been answered, but now he had others. He wondered how much Kate knew. And if she didn't know? Dread crept up his spine. He didn't want to be the one to tell her. But it looked like he had no choice.

Stepping out into the morning sunshine, Brody found Kate waiting on the sidewalk, her arms akimbo and one Italian-loafer-clad foot tapping. His mouth twisted. She was doing a bang-up job of looking like a woman used to getting what she wanted, when she wanted it, but the effort she was putting into the display made him think it wasn't her usual M.O.

The brief summer storm left the air with a crisp

freshness. But the telltale signs of raindrops still beading on his car reminded Brody of the night before and of what Kate would find when she went back to the house. He stopped in his tracks.

"Kate?"

She looked over her shoulder at him, her steps slowing to a halt and her brows drawn together. "Now what?"

"Did you get everything?"

Her brows rose. "I didn't bring anything."

"This, maybe?" He held up her purse.

She snatched it from him. "Thanks," she mumbled.

She wouldn't be thanking him when he told her what he'd discovered. With a pleasureless twist of his lips, he followed her to his cruiser and held open the passenger-side door. She gave him a tight smile and slid in.

As he headed the car down Main Street, he tried to formulate the best way of saying what needed to be said. But every time he tried to tell her, he couldn't get the words to form.

"Okay, out with it."

"Excuse me?"

Kate sighed. "You obviously have something on your mind. You've looked like a fish out of water ever since we got in the car."

He slanted her a glance. "And how is that, exactly?"

"You keep opening your mouth to say something, then shutting it tight." Kate demonstrated with exaggerated movements.

Brody's rich laughter filled the cab of the car. Kate sucked in a breath. She liked the sound of his laugh: deep and warm...and inviting. She forced the thought away. She couldn't let down her guard no matter how pleasing she found the sheriff.

"So, what is it?"

Brody sobered, his expression turning grim. A sense of impending doom filled Kate. What could he possibly have to say that would warrant such a reaction? Nothing, she decided, now that they'd determined she wasn't going to be arrested.

"How long were you married to your...late husband?"

She frowned. "Four years."

"How do you know Pete Kinsey was his business partner?"

That seemed like an odd question. "Paul told me after I found an invoice for a piece of office equipment. It had Kinsey's name on it."

He slanted her a quick glance. "You never met Pete Kinsey?"

She hated the pinprick of hurt needling her. "No. I didn't even know about him until a year ago. Paul hadn't invited anyone he worked with to our wedding."

He didn't comment, as his hands gripped and re-gripped the steering wheel.

"Why?"

He shrugged, then asked, "How well did you know Paul?"

An even odder question.

"As well as one could, I suppose. Paul wasn't your open and friendly type." Thinking back over the course of their relationship, she wondered how she'd missed his coldness in the beginning. Or had he been just that good at hiding it?

"He changed from when you first met him?"

Unnerved that he'd practically read her thoughts, she replied, "Yes, he did."

"He traveled a lot."

It wasn't a question. "Yes. How did you know?"

Without answering, Brody slowed the vehicle and turned down the narrow dirt drive leading to the house.

In the bright morning sun, the cottage-style home and surrounding area held a charming appeal. A far cry from her impression last night. The blue-gray shingles, quaint dormer windows edged in white, and the wrap-around porch were very welcoming. The shrubs and foliage of the yard held a certain rustic charm. And beyond the bungalow, the beach and frothy waves of the Atlantic Ocean gleamed in the sunlight. It was very picturesque and soothing.

Kate wished she'd been able to arrive in the light of day rather than the dead of a stormy night. The late flight out of L.A. and the subsequent drive to Haven-sport had made her arrival untimely.

She regretted she hadn't rented a car instead of arranging for ground transportation. But at the time it seemed the best thing since she hadn't a clue where she was going. Last night, the driver had dropped her off without so much as waiting to see if she'd made it in the house okay, leaving her stranded without any way to get around.

Brody parked and got out. Just as Kate opened the door, he was there offering her his help. She laid her hand in his. Warmth spread up her arm and around her heart. She hadn't felt anything but coldness in so long.

Quickly, she disengaged from him and stepped away. "You didn't answer my question."

"And what question was that?"

She put her hands on her hips. "How did you know Paul traveled?"

Brody ran a hand through his dark hair. She watched the motion with a good dose of curiosity. How would his hair feel beneath her hand? Uncomfortable with the course of her thoughts, she averted her gaze and concentrated on the unseen bird singing from high in the large birch tree to the right of the house.

"I knew your husband."

Snapping to attention, she frowned. "You did?" Wariness coiled tight in her chest. She looked at the house and tried to rationalize how they could have met. "He did own the house even if Pete Kinsey lived here. They were business partners, after all."

"Not partners, exactly."

Apprehension chilled her skin like a cold wind. "Meaning?"

Brody shifted his feet in a restless gesture before saying, "You see, your husband and Pete Kinsey were, well…"

"Yes?"

"Man." His hard jaw tensed. "I'm botching this up."

The wind turned into a full-blown hurricane. Could he have the answers she sought? "What? What should I know?"

Locking his gaze with hers, Brody stated, "They were the same man."

FOUR

She didn't know what she'd expected, but it certainly wasn't something as ridiculous as that. Relief and disappointment made her laugh. "Excuse me?"

"Paul Wheeler and Pete Kinsey were the same person."

She couldn't see any humor in his expression, any mirth glinting in his dark eyes, but she couldn't believe he was serious. "What kind of joke are you trying to play on me, Sheriff?"

"It's no joke."

"Oh, come on." She gave a nervous laugh. "You can't expect me to believe…that…my husband led some sort of…double life."

Brody shrugged. "Believe what you will. The facts speak for themselves."

"What facts?"

Shifting his weight to his left leg, Brody asked, "Was Paul tall, about six feet, with gray eyes and blond hair?"

Mutely, she nodded.

"So was Pete Kinsey."

She scoffed. "Those are your facts?"

Brody's mouth tightened. "Pete Kinsey had a tattoo."

Kate's eyes narrowed. "So?"

"Did Paul?"

"A lot of people have tattoos"

"On their left shoulder?"

Her mouth went dry. "Maybe."

"Shall I describe it to you, Kate?" he asked, gently.

She shrugged and turned away, not liking what she was hearing, what he was insinuating.

"A small broken match."

Her stomach churned. "Tattoos aren't trademarked, Sheriff." She glanced at him and his look told her he thought she was grasping at straws and soon the whole haystack was going to collapse.

"Did you ever go with your husband when he traveled?"

"No. I have my own career to think about."

She almost groaned as the words left her mouth. The bank. This trip put her job, her career, in jeopardy, but she'd needed to take a leave of absence to find the answers to Paul's death. The not knowing was driving her nuts.

And standing here arguing about something this far-fetched wasn't helping her accomplish anything. "Really, Sheriff. I think you should go. Your job here's done."

"Do you know where he went, Kate?"

She rolled her eyes. "His work took him all over the globe."

"And what work was that?"

"He was a financial consultant."

Brody nodded. "He came to the Cape every Fourth of July."

She couldn't say where Paul had gone for sure, and she'd always wondered why he'd work over that holiday. But what the sheriff was saying couldn't be true. Paul was cold, selfish maybe, but he wasn't...

She was about to say he wasn't dishonest, but she knew in her heart that whatever Paul had been mixed up in, it hadn't had anything to do with honesty. But could he have led a double life? No. She would have known, sensed something. Wouldn't she have?

"Goodbye, Sheriff."

He held out a photo. "This is the man I know as Pete Kinsey."

She took the photo, instantly recognizing it. "You must be mistaken."

"I'm not."

She looked up into his eyes and noticed the way a thin, lighter blue ring circled the near-black irises, reminding her of the wind-tossed ocean off the Pacific Northwest coast. The sheriff had no reason to lie to her. But this just couldn't be, her mind insisted. Paul was many things, but was he capable of this kind of deceit?

And if what the sheriff said was true, what did that say about her and her judgment? Could she have been that blind? How could she have been married to a man for four years and not know him?

Somewhere inside the house lay the answers. "This doesn't prove anything."

If it were true that Paul had had another existence, then that made her pretty stupid. Stupid for trusting, for believing in her husband. Stupid for trying so hard to save her marriage even after he'd moved out.

"I…it's just not true."

The look of understanding, of pity, that stole over the sheriff's handsome face made her blood boil.

She crumbled the photo into her fist. "You can go now. I don't need or want you here."

His hand closed over hers. Her gaze was drawn to the way his larger, masculine hand enveloped her smaller, more delicate fingers in a protective grip. Her gaze lifted and met his intense look.

His dark eyes simmered. She could easily fall into the blaze that beckoned and allow herself the luxury of soothing warmth.

"Kate." He spoke her name in an oddly hushed tone.

She jerked her hand away, stunned by the connection and longing welling up inside her.

He stepped back, his expression bemused.

Without another word, she fled to the safety of the house. As she reached the porch, she heard him say, "If you need anything, you know where to find me."

Her steps faltered, and slowly she turned around. Yes, she knew where to find the sheriff. For a moment, she allowed herself the indulgence of looking at him. She noticed the way his uniform outlined his masculine shape; broad chest tapering to a trim waist, long, lean legs.

A spark of sunlight caught her attention. Golden rays glinted off his badge, soaked into his dark hair, and caressed his handsome face. Her hand still tingled where he'd touched her.

Absently she rubbed the spot and took a step backwards, as if the more distance she put between them, the easier it would be to forget the odd sensations she'd felt when they'd touched. Animal attraction. Basic human instinct. God had, after all, gifted humans with the ability to connect physically to another. Though she'd never experienced anything this swift and this profound.

The crumbled ball in her hand bit into her palm and her jaw clenched. Regardless of how her hormones responded to this man, she refused to rely on him for help. She had to find out the truth about Paul on her own. "Goodbye, Sheriff."

His expression rueful, he nodded. She watched him stride back to his car and climb in. He waved his hand in a final salute as he turned the car around. Standing rooted to the porch for several seconds after he had disappeared, a deep loneliness crept over her.

She'd been lonely before. The four years of her marriage were the loneliest in her life, but this sudden intense aloneness rocked her because it was desperate and unfamiliar. How could a man have this much effect on her?

Resolutely, she turned her attention to the house. Inside were the answers. She needed to stay focused and not let herself be distracted by the handsome sheriff.

Squaring her shoulders, she went in.

In the daylight, the house didn't hold such a spooky, haunted-house feel as it had the night before. She looked around and moved purposely into the living room.

Built-in shelves lined one wall; big pieces of furniture covered with sheets dotted the large, dark green area rug.

Drawn to the shelves with the framed pictures, her heart throbbed inside her chest. With a shaky hand, she lifted a frame and stared at the picture. Paul smiled up at her, his arm slung carelessly around a buxom blonde. In the background, blue water sparkled in the glistening sun, mocking her with its seductive invitation to partake of the couple's free and easy spirit.

She dropped the picture. It hit the floor at her feet, the glass cracking in two.

Numbness stole through her, surrounding her heart and chilling her soul as she picked up another frame. In this picture, a party by the looks of it, Paul was flanked on either side by recognizable faces. Some celebrities, others political figures.

Grabbing at another frame, she again saw Paul with famous and well-known people. She plucked at another picture and another until her arms were full. *What is going on?*

It wasn't unreasonable that he would know these people in his line of work. After all, he was a consultant for wealthy people. But why hadn't he mentioned he had the kind of relationship with them that was evident in these pictures?

It was clear that all the photos were taken at the beach house. Some even in the very room she stood in. Her throat constricted and tears blurred her vision as bitterness settled around her like a smothering cloak.

Abruptly, she dumped her load onto the couch. A cloud of dust puffed into the air, little bits and pieces floating away and doing nothing but making her sneeze.

Moving in a fog, Kate went from room to room

looking at the remains of a life cut short. Of a life she'd known nothing about.

Besides the dust, the rooms were clean, uncluttered and devoid of personality. Guest rooms. She came to the room with the broken window. Before nightfall she'd have to have someone come out and repair the damage. She turned away from the reminder of her terror and continued on.

In what appeared to be the master bedroom, she saw signs of Paul—the scent of his cologne clung to the clothes hanging in the closet, his shirts and undergarments folded with precision in the drawers. She swallowed back the vile taste of betrayal.

She found receipts and notes in the top drawer of the oak dresser. The writing was Paul's, but the signature said Pete Kinsey. She stared at the papers. Pain squeezed her head like a vice. How could she have been so oblivious?

The tremors started deep down inside and quickly worked their way out. She sank to her knees and rested her head against the bed. Sobs clogged her throat and tears burned a salty trail down her cheek. Why had Paul, or Pete or whoever he was, lied? Why had he kept a part of himself from her? Was this other identity the reason he'd been killed?

Her hands curved into fists. Why had he involved her?

Lord, I'm so angry and hurt and confused. This doesn't make sense.

A line of scripture floated through her consciousness. *My presence shall go with you, and I will give you rest.*

Clinging to that promise, she slowly crawled up onto the bed and curled into a ball. So tired, so very tired. Her mind shut down and blessed numbness wrapped around her, taking her away from the hurt and endless parade of lies.

Brody's fingers drummed on the desktop. What was Kate's story? The thought had plagued him since he'd left her at the Kinsey house.

"What's eating at you, boss?" Deputy Teal's voice broke through Brody's thoughts.

"Nothing," he replied, absently.

Nothing, everything…Kate. For more hours than he cared to admit to, Brody had been unable to keep his mind off Kate Wheeler. She'd made her feelings clear. And he was glad. He certainly didn't want to be bothered with a headstrong woman who couldn't accept the truth even when it stared her in the face.

Brody stilled his fingers. He'd wasted enough time today thinking about Kate. She wasn't his problem. She owned the house now, and would eventually realize that what he'd told her was the truth and then she'd go back to where she came from. He nodded to close the subject in his mind, but he couldn't quite banish the nagging terror he'd seen in her eyes.

There were other matters needing his attention. Like the feud still raging between Mr. Haskel and Mr. Moore. The two old codgers each swore that the other was poaching fish. Like you could poach fish from the ocean during fishing season.

He shook his head, knowing that the fighting gave

the two widowers something to keep their minds active. Only they sometimes got carried away in their attempts to out-fish each other. On numerous occasions, Brody'd had to settle a dispute over whose fish was whose.

Today it seemed Mr. Haskel had caught Mr. Moore using his lure.

Rolling his chair away from the desk, Brody heard the crinkling sound of paper caught under the wheels. Teal and his paper basketballs. He bent to retrieve what he assumed would be a stray ball and discovered a sheet of fax paper.

He stared at the contents of the fax for a good thirty seconds before he remembered to take a breath.

He knew it. He just knew it. Below the L.A.P.D. heading, the fax stated that Katherine Wheeler was considered a "person of interest" in the murder investigation of Paul Wheeler and that currently Mrs. Wheeler's whereabouts were unknown and she was being sought.

He hoped they were wrong, but if they weren't…

His lip curled. *He* knew where she was. Sitting back down in his chair, he picked up the phone and called California. The line was picked up on the third ring and after Brody explained to the desk sergeant what he wanted, he was transferred to a Detective Arnez.

"Sheriff, what can I do for you?"

Brody swiped a hand through his hair. "I have information concerning the Wheeler investigation."

"Wheeler. Hold on."

Brody heard the rustling of paper before Arnez came back on the line. "Oh, yeah. Got the file right here. Hey, didn't you request the current status of the investigation earlier today?"

"I did."

"So what's your interest?" Arnez asked.

"I don't have an interest," Brody stated quickly. "I caught a perp breaking and entering last night, only it turned out to be Kate Wheeler."

Arnez's voice perked up. "You've got her in custody?"

Brody frowned. "No...I let her go. Her lawyer faxed over the deed to the house and she's the owner. But... I...know where she is." For a reason he couldn't explain, Brody felt as though he was betraying Kate. But that was ridiculous. If she'd committed a crime, she had to pay the price.

"She's in your town, then?" Arnez asked.

"Yes."

"Hold on."

With his free hand Brody drummed his fingers on the desk again as the detective put him on hold. A tight, wound-up feeling stole over him. Had Kate killed her husband? Would he have to arrest her and send her back to L.A.? Why did his mind rebel against the thought? He shook his head, clearing his thoughts.

Concentrate on the job, McClain, nothing else.

He wouldn't think about her copper-colored curls, her big green eyes. None of that mattered. Nor would he think about the vulnerability in her expression, the feisty spirit that he found so appealing. And he definitely wouldn't think about the little dimple on her chin that even now he longed to kiss.

Arnez came back on the line. "Tell you what, Sheriff. The powers that be say keep an eye on her. The case is being handed over to the FBI."

"Why the Feds? Thought this was a simple murder investigation."

"Don't have all the details, but seems the hubby had his fingers in a few pies around the country that he shouldn't have. The Feds are playing this close to the vest, so they'll contact you with further instructions. Just keep tabs on the lady."

"Will do." He wouldn't be arresting Kate again just yet, but he could find out what she knew about her husband's dealings.

After he hung up the phone, he delegated the Haskel/Moore situation to Deputy Teal. Brody left the office, walked the short block to his studio apartment where he changed into a fresh uniform and then headed down the main street of Havensport on foot.

Having spent the night and most of the morning at his desk, it felt good to stretch his legs. His hip hurt, but he was used to the biting pain. Welcomed it, in fact, as a reminder of what getting involved with a woman could do. He wasn't going to get involved with Kate Wheeler, he'd keep things strictly business.

Around him, the small town bustled with energy. After the late-summer squall of the night before, people were busy enjoying the sweet freshness left from the rain. The dress shops and specialty stores had their doors wide open inviting the tourists in, the front of the Book Depot was lined with bins of books. He strode by the Java Stand and inhaled the mouthwatering aromas of baked goods and coffee. He smiled and waved at several locals as a sense of belonging swept through him.

Brody surveyed it all with a sense of pride. He loved Havensport and its people. They'd welcomed him openly when he'd run for the position of sheriff. Not that there had been any other candidates, but still, he'd found a place to belong. A place where people didn't look at him with either pity or mockery.

A movement to the right of his peripheral vision drew his gaze.

Sunlight caught fiery sparks on shoulder-length curls as Kate stepped from the grocery store, her arms laden with bags and a black leather purse slung over her slender shoulder.

She wore a simple but fresh-looking white cotton, button-down blouse and blue jeans that hugged her curves. A tension he hadn't realized he held eased in his chest at the sight of her. He couldn't comprehend the strange sensation, didn't know where it was coming from or why. He only knew that on some level he was drawn to her, to her spirit that kindled something deep inside him.

Man, she was beautiful. Not in a classic model way, not the way Elise had been beautiful. No, Kate was the girl-next-door kind of beauty. The type a guy could get cozy with, feel at home with, snuggled up close in front of a roaring fire with, her head resting on his chest… Brody shook off the image. He couldn't let himself fall into that trap. *Keep it professional, McClain.*

He'd been asked to keep an eye on her and that's what he would do. Nothing more.

The loud screech of tires split the air. A dark blue van barreled down the road toward the mercantile. Abruptly, the vehicle slowed as it neared the shop. The side door slid open and the van halted directly in front of Kate. A man wearing a black ski mask leapt out. His hands closed around Kate's upper arms as he dragged her toward the open door. The bags she held fell to the ground. Milk splattered over the hot pavement, an orange rolled under the van.

Kate's scream ripped Brody's senses apart.

Brody ran with one hand pulling his sidearm from the holster at his hip.

"Stop," He shouted at the top of his lungs.

The masked man paused and looked at him. Killer's eyes. Cold and hard. Brody'd seen eyes like that before. The man who'd killed his father had those same type of eyes.

The frantic motions of the driver, whose face was also obscured by a mask, spurred the first man back into action. Kate struggled against her captor as he continued to drag her toward the vehicle.

Brody raised his weapon. The van's engine roared. Having no other option, Brody planted a warning shot through the side of the van.

The man holding Kate shoved her aside before jumping back into the vehicle just as the van vaulted forward, the tires burning black smoke against the street. The van swerved toward Brody. He dove to the side, his body hitting hard on the sidewalk before he rolled to safety.

Ignoring the explosion of pain in his hip, he raised his weapon, aimed and fired again. A taillight exploded from the impact of his bullet. In frustration, Brody watched the van peel around a corner and disappear.

"Great." He picked himself up off the ground. His hip throbbed, the pain ricocheting down his whole right side. He limped over to Kate.

She sat in the flowerbed in front of the store. The shocked expression on her face didn't hide the terror in her eyes.

Brody painfully hunkered down in front of her. "Kate. Kate, talk to me."

Her gaze lifted. Tears welled in her eyes and her lower lip trembled. "Are they gone?"

"Yes." He gathered her close and helped her to her feet.

"My…my groceries," she whispered, pulling away from him. She bent and picked up the mess lying in the road.

Brody firmly took her hands, stopping her movements. Her body shook violently. Shock was setting in. Brody's gut tightened. She was vulnerable and in need of his protection. He led her to a bench. "Come on, Kate. Over here. Sit down."

"Here, Sheriff," Myrtle Kirby, the mercantile's owner, handed him a blanket. He wrapped it around Kate's shoulders, his hands lingering, offering comfort.

"Kate, sit here. I'm going to hunt those men down."

"Don't leave." Kate grabbed his hand and held on tightly, her eyes begging him to stay.

Her hand was ice cold. He wanted to pull her close and wrap her in his embrace and tell her everything would be okay. He didn't.

"I'll sit with her, Sheriff," Myrtle volunteered. "But she needs a drink of water after what those nasty men tried to do."

Pulling his hand from Kate's, Brody nodded his thanks to the older woman and watched her walk briskly back inside. Unnerved by Kate's pleading gaze and his own reluctance to leave her, Brody turned his back and paced a few steps away. It was too late to follow the van, anyway. Using the radio attached to his uniform, he contacted Deputy Teal.

"Warren, I want you to get an APB out on a dark blue van." Brody gave the model and make. Not surprisingly, the license plates had been removed.

"Okay, boss. What's up?"

"Occupants attempted to kidnap Kate Wheeler."

"Wow, when did this happen?"

Brody's grip on the radio tightened. "Warren, just do it now."

"Okay, okay."

"Sheriff!" Myrtle cried from the doorway of the little store.

Turning sharply, Brody's heart slammed into his throat. The blanket lay in a heap on the ground and Kate Wheeler was nowhere in sight.

He'd been duped again. So much for the damsel-in-distress routine. He was going to find her and make her talk even if he had to haul her back to jail.

FIVE

Kate kept running despite the stitch in her side.

Run. Run. Run.

Over and over, the single word replayed itself inside her head. Her lungs ached and her muscles burned. And still she ran, her sneakers making a thwacking noise against the still-damp pavement and her purse banging against her side.

The house. She had to get to the house where she could hide and watch, and maybe finally see what it was *they* were after.

With every pounding step, her terror was giving way to anger. Because of Paul and the mess he'd left her in, her life was threatened, her career possibly lost and her heart numbed. To think she'd given four years of her love and her life to him only to have been betrayed so thoroughly. And the betrayal continued, even in his death.

With no sign of the van, she bounded up the porch stairs. Her feet skidded to a halt and she widened her eyes in shock. Wood splintered around the busted lock on the front door. A shiver ran the course of her body.

Idiot, you're too late. You'll never learn the truth.

Kate spun around, her gaze searching the area. No one lurked behind the stand of trees off to the right and the path leading around the house toward the beach lay deserted.

Even the house across the way appeared uninhabited. She seemed to be alone. Should she go in? Should she run back to town? Did it even matter?

She was suddenly overwhelmed with the knowledge that she was alone and so utterly at a loss as to what to do. Were the men inside the house waiting for her? Or had they already come and gone? Her shoulders sagged.

Okay, think. Logic suggested that they'd come and gone. And obviously not found what they were looking for or they wouldn't have tried to kidnap her. She clenched her fists. She wished she knew what she was supposed to have.

She placed her hand over her runaway heart. "Okay...that would mean, for the moment, I'm relatively safe and no closer to answers." She cringed as the last word hung in the salty breeze.

Suddenly, the crash of the ocean was overshadowed with the roar of an engine, the sound of tires eating up the gravel. The hairs on the back of her neck stood up. Kate whirled around, ready to bolt, and nearly fainted with relief at the sight of the sheriff's car as it slid to a halt.

Sheriff McClain leapt out of the vehicle and covered the distance between them in long, angry strides. "Just what do you think you're doing?"

"Don't yell at me."

He visibly reined in his anger, taking a deep breath

and slowly exhaling. His too-dark gaze bored into hers. "I told you to stay put."

"I…I just…just couldn't sit there." Didn't he understand? It wasn't in her nature to let life happen. She had to do something, and running for the house was the only thing she could think of.

"What if those men had been here when you arrived?" He made a chopping gesture with his hands. "Did you even think of that?"

"They weren't here."

"But they could have been."

Touched by his concern, she lowered her voice. "But they weren't. They'd already been here and gone."

His eyes narrowed. "How do you know?"

She stepped aside and pointed to the broken lock on the door.

"Oh, man," he muttered.

Striding past her, he inspected the lock. With the tip of his shoe he pushed opened the door while he withdrew his weapon from his holster.

"They aren't here," she repeated.

He shot her a hard look before taking her by the arm and propelling her back down the stairs to his cruiser.

"What…what are you doing?"

He released her to open the car door. "Calling in a CSI team."

"Don't bother. I seriously doubt they'll find anything useful."

"This a crime scene."

She pinned him with her gaze. "There's no crime if I don't report it."

His mouth twisted. "Consider it already reported."

Exasperated, she spread out her hands. "I couldn't begin to know if anything is missing."

He dipped his chin and gave her a look of disbelief. "You didn't explore the house?"

"A little." She didn't want to confess she'd been so shaken by the revelation of Paul's double life that she'd spent several hours in a stupor before finally shaking it off. To escape the house and its contents, she'd gone for a walk along the ocean before heading into town for supplies.

"I'm not going to have you bring a bunch of people traipsing through here." She jabbed a finger at him, even though deep down she knew she was being ridiculous. She didn't even like the house. "I still have rights, you know."

He gave her a grim smile. "True. You have the right to stay out of the way."

"You are insufferable," she huffed.

One dark brow lifted. "I aim to please, ma'am."

Realizing any more protests would be useless, Kate folded her arms over her chest, leaned against the front end of the car and settled in to wait.

Later, in what felt to Kate like an interminably long time, but which in actuality was two hours, the crime scene investigators had come, done their job and taken whatever information they'd gathered away.

"Satisfied?" Kate asked as Brody rejoined her at the car.

He shrugged. "We'll see. Are you ready to go back in?"

Ready? If she never set foot inside again she'd be happy. But that wasn't to be, so she pushed away from the car. "Let's see what damage has been done."

Careful not to touch the black powder dusted on the door lock and frame, Kate stepped into the living room. The place looked as if a tornado had touched down. The shelves were in disarray, glass littered the rug, white stuffing protruded from the couch and loveseat, and books were strewn about the floor.

Not again. Kate's heart plummeted to her toes. Even though the house had only been in her possession for a short time, she felt violated. The feeling left a bitter taste in her mouth. "Those dirty, rotten...oh!"

She found her nose jammed into the sheriff's broad back. The freshly laundered scent of his brown uniform shirt brought order to the chaos surrounding her.

"Steady there," he said as his hands settled on her shoulders.

He anchored her, made her feel safe. She moved away from him. "Sorry," she mumbled, disconcerted now by her reaction to him.

She preceded him down the hall. Each room looked the same as the living room. Nothing had been left untouched or intact.

Anger grew with each breath she took. How dare those men tear apart what was left of Paul's life? It wasn't fair. But then again, it wasn't fair of Paul to involve her in his shady dealings.

She shuddered to think what would have happened had she been here when the men had come in. She wouldn't have thought it possible, but she was suddenly very grateful she'd spent the night in jail. If she hadn't, she wouldn't now have the sheriff's protection.

"Kate, what were they looking for?"

His sudden question forced her thoughts to focus. "I...I don't know."

Her mind toyed with telling him of Paul's dying words, but the memory of the suspicion in the L.A.P.D. detective's eyes stopped her cold. That man hadn't believed her, had even insinuated that she'd killed Paul. Would the sheriff react the same way?

"Look, Kate. Until you level with me, I can't help you."

Help. The word conjured up a sense of welcomed relief. But how far should she trust this man? Granted, he'd saved her life and he seemed sincerely concerned, but was that enough? Would he believe her? "Sheriff McClain..."

"Brody," he said, his voice low and husky.

She ducked her head as heat rose in her cheeks and a smile curved her lips. "All right then...Brody." For the life of her, she didn't understand her reaction. She was blushing like a fourteen-year-old.

The hallway became too confining, the sheriff too close and big. Needing some distance, she stepped past Brody and walked back into the living room. Glass crunched beneath her shoes, the sound echoed in her heart.

Behind her, she could feel Brody's presence like a buffer from the storm. She realized she wanted to trust him, to confide in him the horror of finding Paul's body, the terror of not knowing why or from whom she was in danger.

"Kate, talk to me. Tell me what's going on."

Suddenly cold, she wrapped her arms around herself. "I honestly don't know what's happening." She turned to look at him. The heat in his eyes could warm her. "It seems you were right about Paul being Pete Kinsey."

Contrition filled Brody's face. "I'm sorry you had to find out like this."

"Me, too." Kate bent to pick up a torn photo. She stared at her husband. Who had he really been? "I found him."

Brody stepped closer. "What?"

Tears blurred her vision. The image in the photo swam out of focus. "After they…hurt him. I…I found him."

"Who are they?" Brody's gently asked question came from very near her shoulder.

She shook her head. She didn't have the answer to that question. "He…he told me I was in danger. He…he said…he—" A sob clogged her throat.

Warm hands descended to her shoulders and slowly turned her around. "Who are they?" he repeated.

"I don't know," she whispered to the front of his shirt.

The slight pressure of his hand raising her chin sent tremors rippling over her skin. She sucked in a sharp breath when she met his gaze. Deep in the depths of his eyes, just beyond his concern, lurked suspicion. Kate saw it, acknowledged it and hated it. She had to make him believe in her.

"Brody, I don't know what Paul was involved in. I don't know why he was killed or…or who's after me."

His expression shifted slightly, became colder, more remote.

Almost desperately, Kate tried again. "You…you've got to listen to me." She fisted her hand in his shirt. "I

want answers just as badly as you do. Don't you see…
it's my life that's in danger? Do you really think if I
knew who'd killed Paul…I wouldn't tell the police?"

For the briefest of seconds his eyes flickered with in-
decision. She grasped on to a moment of hope.

"Please…please believe me."

She didn't understand when it had become so important that he believe her, but suddenly it was. God had
brought Brody into her life and if Brody, who seemed
so sure of himself, so confident and secure, could
believe in her, then surely she'd be able to get out of the
predicament that Paul's death had left her in.

Brody stepped away from her and her heart nearly
crumbled. His demeanor turned rigid and unbending.
"I'd like to believe you, Kate. But somehow your words
don't ring completely true. You're hiding something. I'd
like to know what."

Disappointment rolled in, but she refused to give it
any ground. Instead, she shifted the conversation. "I
haven't thanked you for saving me today."

His gaze narrowed. "Why did you need saving?"

She clenched her jaw, controlling the rising exaspera-
tion. "I don't know, but I'm thankful you were there."

"Doing my job."

"No, it was more than that. You were at the right
place at the right time."

He shrugged. "Coincidence."

"I don't believe in coincidence. God put you where
you needed to be."

Brody moved to the door with a frown etched in his
forehead. "I'll have someone come out and fix that lock."

She allowed him to dodge her statement. He clearly didn't want to go there. She stepped to the door and touched the bent metal. "I don't think replacing the lock will stop them from coming back."

"No. It won't." His dark, intense gaze bored into her. "Kate, I—"

"Look, Sheriff." She cut him off, resigned to not having his trust or his help. "Your job here's done. You can go."

He stared at her for a long, taut moment, then nodded and left, leaving Kate alone again. Disappointment twisted around her like ivy vines, almost choking her, but she shoved the disappointment away. She couldn't rely on him.

She leaned against the closed, broken door and wished she'd never come to Havensport looking for answers. But without the answers, the unknown would always haunt her and keep her from the things she needed most: peace and security.

"No," she cried to the empty house and kicked the door with her heel.

She refused to give in to defeat. She'd seen what allowing despair and hopelessness did to her mother. No way was she going to let it happen to her.

Take charge was Kate's motto. Don't let life happen to you, make it happen *for* you.

She pushed away from the door and stormed into the living room. Who needed the sheriff anyway? She certainly didn't. She'd find the truth on her own. She'd prove to him that she was innocent even if it killed her.

She snorted. It just might.

A chill zigzagged down her back. Quickly she spun around, half expecting to see two masked men come bursting through the broken door. No one was there.

She needed to find a weapon, something with which to defend herself with if they did return.

In the kitchen, she found a large carving knife and then headed for the living room.

Staring at the shambles the intruders had left in their wake, she wondered what they'd been looking for. And why hadn't they found it?

The chaos surrounding her made her edgy. She didn't like it when life wasn't in order. It drove her nuts not to have one plus two equal three.

And nothing had been adding up since she'd walked into their apartment and discovered Paul.

Kate laid the knife on a side table next to a brass lamp and pushed the stuffing back into the gaping hole in the middle of the navy-and-white striped couch.

Why couldn't Brody have given her the benefit of the doubt?

She punched the stuffing, the rough fiber rasping against her fist.

Why had he, like the other detective, assumed she had something to do with Paul's murder?

She slammed her fist into the material again, leaving a dent. Flopping back onto the couch, she acknowledged the pent-up adrenaline still pumping through her veins.

Calm down. Take deep breaths. Imagine yourself on a tropical sandy beach.

The self-talk wasn't working. Her muscles were bunched and wound tight. Her heart still beat faster than normal and her jaw ached, giving testimony to the headache brewing.

Sudden footsteps on the stairs broke the stillness of the house.

She sprang up from the couch and swiped the knife off the table.

The footsteps trailed across the porch and approached the door.

Renewed adrenaline flooded through Kate. Blood roared in her ears.

The masked men had returned.

She positioned herself beside the door. Knife ready, she held her breath and waited for the intruder to burst in.

A loud knock reverberated against the wood.

"Who is it?" she barked.

"McClain."

She released a compressed breath and relaxed her stance. Still cautious, she opened the door a crack and peered out.

The sheriff indeed stood there.

Ignoring the ridiculous surge of pleasure, Kate stated flatly, "I thought you'd left."

Brody's expression turned serious. "Until those men are caught, you're under my protection."

"So you're here because its part of your job," Kate stated. Why did that thought irritate her?

He gave her a bland look. "Yes, Kate, protecting you is part of my job." He inclined his head toward the door. "May I?"

Kate pulled her bottom lip between her teeth. She

wanted to say no, go away. She'd already decided she didn't need him or his protection, yet deep inside a little voice whispered, *let him do his job.* Kate opened the door wider and stepped aside.

Brody stepped into the entryway and Kate noticed how much space he took up. It seemed as if the very air around him expanded and grew with the force of his presence. The house didn't seem lonely with him there.

Kate stifled a laugh at her own absurdity.

"Get your things together."

She gaped. "Excuse me?"

"You can't stay here. Myrtle has an empty room she'll let you stay in."

Annoyed at his high-handedness, she huffed. "I'm not leaving."

"Look, you can't stay here." His gaze narrowed to dark, intimidating slits as he closed the distance between them.

Engulfed by his nearness, her pulse accelerated. She knew the rush of sensation whizzing through her had nothing to do with fear and everything to do with him as a man. An attractive man. She swallowed hard.

In a sudden movement, he clutched her wrist and held her arm upright.

The carving knife glinted between them, bringing reality sharply into focus.

SIX

Mortification flushed through Kate. Her gaze darted to his and locked on. He arched a dark brow. He knew. In the swirling dark depths of his eyes, she saw the thread connecting the knife she now held to the weapon used in Paul's murder.

Deftly, he took possession of the weapon.

"I...I had to defend my...myself. I didn't...you left." She decided the best defense was a good offense. "You left. I was alone. I reached for the first thing that came to mind."

"Interesting that a knife should come to mind."

Kate flinched. "What else was I to do? Those men could've come back and you weren't here."

"I was here, Kate. Just outside."

Her heart gave a little lurch. He hadn't left her. "But I didn't know that."

He nodded slightly, before stepping past her to the dining table where he laid the knife down. "You know a knife isn't a good weapon for anyone, let alone a woman to use," he said, conversationally. "Too easy for it to be taken away and used against you." He met her gaze. "For future reference."

Unnerved by that little tidbit, she frowned. "Look, Sheriff McClain. I…"

"Brody."

He leaned against the table and folded his arms across his chest. His cotton uniform shirt stretched over defined biceps emphasizing his physical strength. She swallowed against the longing to have those solid arms wrapped around her, shielding her from danger. Uncomfortable with her thoughts, as well as once again being given permission to use his first name, she began again. "Brody. I didn't kill my husband."

"Then why did you run from L.A.?"

She frowned, feeling somehow that she was walking into a trap. "I didn't run."

"Weren't you informed that you shouldn't leave town?"

"Well…yes. I mean…right after it happened, that detective told me to stick close to home in case they had more questions. But…that was forever ago. Surely I don't need to still be there."

"You're considered a person of interest in the case and until you're exonerated from the investigation, you should've stayed put."

"I didn't know." That must have been why Gordon had advised her not to leave.

"So what *do* you know?"

"Nothing. I know nothing." *I told them you have it, Kate. Trust no one.*

She'd tried to trust the police in L.A. That had gotten

her nowhere. Detective Arnez and his insinuations left her feeling totally stranded.

All right, Mrs. Wheeler. You meet your husband with divorce papers in hand. He's not so anxious to sign. Maybe doesn't want to give you everything you're asking for. You get angry, maybe even a little nuts. You grab a knife and stab him to death.

Kate blinked up at the detective in horror. *No, that didn't happen.*

Oh, come on now. It happens all the time. The wifey gets hacked and then hacks the hubby.

I want my lawyer. Kate stared at the cold metal table then up at the mirrored wall. *I want my lawyer.*

Yeah, yeah. I know. He's coming.

Kate closed her eyes to the scene, trying to block out the bitter taste of the detective's suspicion. It wasn't fair. She'd done everything right. She hadn't touched anything save Paul and the phone. She'd called 911. Why did everyone want her to be guilty?

A tear leaked from the corner of her eye and trickled down her cheek. The roughened pad of Brody's finger glided across her skin and caught the tear.

Kate's eyes snapped open at the unexpected contact. In hypnotic fascination, she watched him rub the wetness between his index finger and thumb. A shiver traipsed down her spine, leaving her breathless.

She met his dark, smoldering gaze. Her knees loosened, and her breathing turned shallow. His full lips drew her gaze.

Abruptly, Brody stepped back. Cooling air filled the space between them. Like a door slammed shut, Brody's eyes became shuttered and his expression closed, unreadable. He spun on his heel and strode into the living room.

Kate sagged against the table. What had just happened?

She forced her breathing to a slow inhale and exhale. No. No. No. She wouldn't allow herself to be attracted to him. No way, no how. Attraction, emotions, feelings. They were distractions that would only keep her from finding the truth.

The tips of her fingers grazed the sharp edge of the knife lying on the table. She jerked away and stared at the prism of light reflecting off the blade. The sheriff didn't believe her.

The man had nearly accused her of murder.

But he'd trusted her enough to leave the knife lying unguarded, and she couldn't deny the yearning inside to lean on him. None of it made sense. She'd never reacted to a man in such a manner before, not even Paul.

She loathed the chaos going on inside her head, twisting up her emotions, making her see things in the sheriff's eyes that couldn't possibly be there.

She forced her feet to move, to carry her to the living room where Brody was stacking the ruined picture frames. His fingers carefully picked through the glass and debris.

Maybe if she concentrated on the chaos of the house and put it in order the rest would follow suit. With purposeful steps she headed to the bookshelf.

"Did you grow up in L.A.?"

Brody's causally asked question grabbed her attention. "No. I grew up in a small town in Washington state."

Brody nodded. "I've never been to that side of the country. I imagine it's beautiful."

"Yes, it is." She started picking up books from the floor. "A beauty that I'd never appreciated until I'd moved to southern California."

"Is that where you met Paul?"

"Is this an interrogation?" she countered tightly.

When no reply came, Kate glanced up to find Brody's intense gaze locked on her.

"No, Kate. I was just curious."

"Oh." She smiled sheepishly. "Sorry."

Brody began picking up the strewn magazines off the floor. "What took you to L.A.?"

"School."

"Where?"

She smoothed the pages of a hardback fiction book. "I received a scholarship to UCLA."

"That's a long way from home." Brody bent to pick up a rectangle of paper from the floor.

She shrugged and watched his blunt fingers rub the edge of a business card. "It got me away from my mother and gave me a purpose. Something to work towards."

He tucked the card into the front pocket of his shirt. "Why did you want to get away from your mother?"

She reached for another book. "My mother…has problems."

There was a moment of silence and Kate was glad he didn't ask for more about her mother.

Brody righted a chair. "Do your parents still live in that small town?"

Kate paused as she reached for more books. "My mother does. My father is retired in Florida."

"Divorce?"

Nodding, she picked up more books and arranged them on the shelf. Maybe if she opened up and let him see who she was, then maybe she could win his trust. "I was fifteen when my father walked out."

"That's rough." Brody commented softly.

"You have no idea." She couldn't quite keep the bitterness out of her voice.

"Messy, huh?" Compassion filled Brody's tone.

"My father was career military. Special Ops. Onward and upward was his motto. Mom and I got tired of the constant moving. Mom pleaded with him to take a post in one place long enough for me to complete high school. His solution was to leave us behind."

"Must have been hard on you."

She shrugged, belying the hurt of her father's desertion. "Not as hard as it was on Mom."

"Meaning?"

She swallowed back the bitterness, the anger directed at her father, at his dedication to the job. "My mom spent so many years living in fear of losing Dad. Years of finding him gone in the middle of the night on some mission, never knowing if he'd return and if he did would he be hurt? When dad finally bugged out, Mom slipped into a deep depression and found solace in the bottle."

The compassion in Brody's eyes sent her heart pounding against her ribs. "I'm sorry, Kate."

With a shrug she dismissed his sympathy. "Yeah, well. I tried to pick someone unlike my father. Someone safe. Risk-free. I mean, how much more stable and normal could I get than a financial consultant?" She laughed at the irony. "Look where that got me."

"Some risks you can't foresee."

"Right." She tracked Brody's movement to the couch. His hand traced the dent in the stuffing left by her fist. Goose bumps raised along her flesh. What would his caress feel like?

She rubbed her arms and pushed the ridiculous question away. "And you, Brody? You a native of Havensport?"

"No."

The one-word answer conjured up a ton of questions, but Kate didn't ask. She didn't want to know this man, didn't want to get too close and start to care. She might not be able to foresee all risks, but there were some risks she could avoid.

"What do you plan to do with this place?" he asked.

She thought about that. She certainly wouldn't be living here, her life was back in L.A. and keeping it as a vacation home didn't seem right. She doubted she'd ever relax here. This was Paul's, not hers. "I'll sell it."

He nodded and made a sweeping gesture with his hand. "And all this stuff?"

"Box it up and give it away. I don't want any of it."

"Sounds like a plan. We can get some boxes from the mercantile." He glanced at his watch. "Let's get you settled at Myrtle's first. We can deal with this tomorrow."

Though she was grateful for his willingness to help, she wondered what he saw as he stared at her with his dark, hooded eyes. Could he see her wounded heart? Did he realize how difficult this all was for her? Could she handle compassion from a guy like him?

Only one thing to do. Shore up her defenses against any compulsion to lean on him. She'd get through this. God would help her.

She lifted her purse from the floor by the front door. As she left the little bungalow by the ocean, she wished she could as easily leave the past behind.

It would be a long while before she could put Paul's memory to rest. She only hoped she didn't end up following him into the grave.

Myrtle's white lap-sided house with its weathered cedar-shingled overhang sat on a side street right off Main Street. An easy walk from the mercantile store and not far from the sheriff's station. An old Stars and Stripes hung from a pole on the corner of the house. The front door opened and Myrtle stepped out to greet Brody and Kate as they neared the porch.

"Oh, you sweet thing, I was so worried about you." Myrtle slipped an arm around Kate and drew her into the small two-bedroom home.

Brody followed them in and set Kate's suitcases near the door. Amused, he watched color flood Kate's cheeks. He'd been on the receiving end of Myrtle's good-natured mothering before. Watching the gray-haired woman hover over Kate made him think of his own mother.

He made a mental note to call home to check on her and see what trouble his siblings were in because there was always some crisis going on.

"You nearly gave me a heart attack today, young lady," Myrtle gently admonished as she led Kate to the overstuffed flowery couch in the small living room.

Light from the smoldering fire in the stone fireplace caught in Kate's hair and made her curls shine like a bright new penny. She had the grace to look contrite. "I'm sorry. I never meant to alarm you."

"Well, it's a good thing our dear sheriff was able to find you. Whatever made you take off like that?" Myrtle gave her a pointed look, her gently lined face stern, yet concern shone in her intelligent gray eyes.

This should be interesting. Brody arched a brow, waiting for Kate's answer.

Kate slanted him a quick glance. "I wanted to see if I could find out what those men were after."

Brody's jaw clenched. So, she hadn't been running to the house for safety like he'd first thought. Didn't she have any idea how much danger she could have been in?

But then again, maybe she was lying. Maybe she'd planned this whole event to throw suspicion off herself, to cover up the fact that she'd killed her husband. The possibility tied his insides up in knots.

There was something about her. Maybe it was the way she spoke about God with such conviction that made him want to believe her.

He rubbed his chin, ignoring the sick feeling settling in the pit of his stomach. She'd gained a measure of his trust after the attempted kidnapping, but the small grain of trust receded to nothing more than a speck as a strange sense of déjà vu seeped into his bones.

He'd been down this road before and he wouldn't make the same mistake he'd made with Elise. Her innocence had been a sham he'd too easily bought and paid the price for.

Kate's words about God could be just that. Words.

"What *were* those men after, Kate?" he asked, hoping to catch her off guard.

She started at his question, a flash of…something in her expression. Guilt? "I don't know."

"So you've said." His gut told him she was hiding something. His wariness grew, but he was a patient man. Time would reveal the truth. The best way to keep an eye on her was to keep her with him.

But he resisted the idea.

He still had a town to serve and he'd made it a policy years ago not to take civilians on calls. He'd learned the hard way what horrors could be witnessed. The dangers the unsuspecting could be made to suffer or, worse yet, the distraction that could cost a life. She'd be safe with Myrtle. Moving to the door, he said, "Ladies, I'll return later to see how you're doing."

Kate shook her head. "That won't be necessary. You've done your job here. I can manage."

"Just the same. I'll be back."

She shrugged and turned away.

As he left Myrtle's, he decided to have Warren camp out front, in case Kate's kidnappers returned or she decided to run.

A little voice in his head warned him not to be surprised if she did take off. Kate was a woman who had secrets. Was her innocent routine an act? Did she have something to do with her husband's death? Who were the men who'd tried to grab her? Did she have ties to them?

He thought about the story she'd told of her father and the reason she'd married Paul. She'd claimed to want a safe, risk-free life. Yet she'd come clear across the country to find answers about her husband's death.

It seemed to him the safe, risk-free thing for her to do would be to sit back and let the authorities do their job. She was a puzzle he'd like to solve.

So many questions. No answers. Yet. Waiting and watching was the key. She'd trip herself up eventually. Then he'd know whether she was a good actress or an innocent victim.

Too bad he didn't know which to hope for.

"Here, dear. Make yourself at home," Myrtle showed Kate to the spare bedroom. "If you need anything, let me know."

Grateful for the older woman's kindness, Kate smiled. "Thank you so much. I hope I'm not imposing."

Myrtle waved a hand. "Oh, please. Not at all."

The jingle of the phone drew Myrtle away, leaving Kate alone in the small room with a colorful patchwork quilt covering the full-size bed and a dark oak dresser against one wall.

Everything about Myrtle's house was warm and comforting. Very much like Kate's memories of her grandmother. Antiques and lace doilies, things that spoke of a different era, made Kate long for the simplicity of being with her maternal grandmother, the only person whose love she'd never doubted.

On some level, she knew her parents loved her. She was their only child. But her father had been devoted to his career, her mother to her father, then to the bottle. When her husband had left, Constance Hyde had slowly slipped into alcoholic oblivion, leaving Kate feeling helpless and insecure.

Helpless. Insecure.

Feelings she'd fought and had thought she'd conquered. She was an independent woman with an upwardly mobile career that had prestige and responsibility and she'd once had a dream husband.

But that was the problem. Paul had been a dream, an illusion, and she'd been so blind. Looking for the fairy-tale ending of happily ever after that now she suspected didn't really exit. Her parents certainly hadn't found it and neither had she.

Wanting to do something productive to stop her depressing thoughts, Kate went in search of Myrtle. She found her in the living room, just finishing her phone call.

"Myrtle, would the mercantile have empty boxes I could have?" Now was as good a time as any to box up Paul's life.

"Of course, dear." Myrtle smiled. "Let's walk over there."

As they left the house, Kate noticed a sheriff's car parked down the street. The car was slightly different than the one Brody drove and she could see Deputy Teal behind the wheel. So Brody was having her watched. For protection or because he didn't trust her?

She wouldn't waste her time trying to figure out his motives.

They walked the three blocks to the mercantile. Kate liked the quaint town with its rustic charm and sleepy pace. There were no rushing cars or hurrying pedestrians too busy even to smile as they passed by. The few cars on the street rolled by slowly and the spattering of foot traffic moved at a sedate pace. Kate inhaled the salty scent of the ocean and listened to the soothing sound of the waves.

Life in Havensport seemed uncomplicated and tranquil. She longed for the peace of such a life.

At the mercantile, she gathered up several empty boxes. Myrtle arranged to have the boxes delivered and left on the porch of Kate's cottage. Then as they walked back toward Myrtle's, Kate had an idea. "Would you mind if I walk over to the bank?"

Concern crinkled at the corners of Myrtle's eyes. "You'll be careful?"

"Yes," she replied. She wouldn't be caught unaware again.

"Don't be long, dear. I'll fix us something to eat."

They separated and Kate headed toward the First National Bank. In the style of most of Havensport, the bank had cedar shingles that had been stained to a red-gold color. Baskets of multicolored flowers hung from the large roof overhang. Inside, plush beige carpeting, soothing peach-colored walls and gleaming fixtures made a welcoming atmosphere. Kate headed to the nearest desk and asked to see the manager.

A tall man in a brown business suit came out from a windowed office. He had nicely styled blond hair and a warm smile. He extended his hand. "I'm Andy Sheldon, the manager. What can I do for you?"

"Hopefully, you can tell me if my husband had an account here and if he had a safe deposit box."

The man's brows rose. "Well, let's see what we can do."

Kate followed the man back to his office. She could only hope her quest for answers would stop here. Then she could leave Havensport and the sheriff with his suspicions behind.

"Sheriff?"

Brody pressed the button on the radio attached to his shoulder. "Yes, Teal?"

"The ladybird left the mercantile and headed into the bank. You want me to go in there? See what she's up to?"

Brody shook his head at the deputy's corny lingo. "No. Sit tight."

Shutting off the computer, Brody left the station and headed down the street to the bank. He had run a check on Kate, on Paul Wheeler and on Pete Kinsey and had found nothing new. No priors. No outstanding parking tickets even. On the surface everything looked on the up and up. Relief filtered through him, catching him off guard. He hadn't realized how much he'd been expecting to find something shady in her past.

He walked inside the bank just as Kate was walking out of Andy Sheldon's office. Brody stepped off to the side next to the door beside a ficus tree. Kate and Andy shook hands and then she headed toward the door.

Her shoulders were slightly slumped and her expression pensive. It wasn't until she was reaching for the door that she noticed him. She started. "What are you doing here?"

"Keeping an eye on you."

"Worried I might rob the bank?" she asked sarcastically before pushing through the door.

He caught her by the elbow as they stepped outside. "Worried someone will try to grab you again." He didn't add that he was also having her watched because he didn't completely trust her.

Her mouth tightened at the corners. "I appreciate your diligence in doing your job, but this is overkill. Those men aren't going to come back."

"You don't know that," he countered. Or did she? "What did you find out at the bank?"

She let out a heavy sigh. "Nothing. Neither Paul nor Pete had an account or safe deposit box there."

"Back to square one," he murmured.

She started walking. He fell into step with her. They headed back toward Myrtle's. "Yes. Back to not knowing anything more than I did this morning." She kicked at a rock lying in the road and sent it scuttling into the bushes. "I had some boxes taken over to the house."

"Good. The window will be repaired by this evening. First thing tomorrow I'll take you over and help you pack up."

"Anxious to get rid of me?" she asked drily as she stepped onto Myrtle's porch.

To be honest with himself…yeah, he did want to send her on her way as quickly as possible. He didn't like this conflicted nonsense going on inside of him. "Just trying to be of service," he replied. "I'll see you tomorrow."

She gave him a tight smile and then disappeared inside.

As Brody returned to the station, he thought about Kate's question. He wished he didn't suspect he'd miss her when she disappeared from his life for good.

SEVEN

Kate awoke feeling refreshed from a good night's sleep. For the second time in as many days she'd not had a nightmare. She supposed it was because she felt safe at Myrtle's with Deputy Teal just down the road.

She peeked out her bedroom window that looked out at the street. Sure enough, there was a car down the road, but it wasn't Deputy Teal's car.

It was Brody's.

A tingling of anticipation raced through her system. She tried to subdue the sudden pleasure of knowing that Brody was the one watching over her.

Irritated with herself for such ridiculousness, she quickly dressed and left the room. Being pleased that Brody was watching over her really shouldn't make any difference.

The smell of bacon and coffee scented the air and made her stomach rumble. She hadn't had much of an appetite the previous night and had only eaten a little of the chicken and rice Myrtle had made.

Kate walked into the kitchen as Myrtle was putting

a plate piled high with bacon into the oven. "Good morning," Kate said.

Myrtle straightened and wiped her hands on the red-checkered apron tied at her waist. "Morning, dear. Sleep well?"

"I did. Thank you."

"Whenever you're ready for breakfast, there's bacon in the oven, eggs in the warmer." She pointed to a covered silver dish. A flame heated the metal bottom. Obviously Myrtle was used to entertaining. "Cups are there." She pointed to a cup rack on the wall by the refrigerator where several mugs hung. "Would you care to join me at church this morning?"

A longing to be in a place where God was present welled inside Kate. The necessity to replenish her faith was strong. "Yes. I'd love that."

"Wonderful. The service starts in an hour and a half." Myrtle picked up a sponge and wiped down the counter.

"Would you mind if I take a cup of coffee to Sheriff McClain?"

Myrtle's brows drew together creating more creases in her forehead. "The sheriff's here?"

"Outside in his car."

Myrtle put the sponge down in the sink and then went to the front window. "Was he there all night?"

Kate shrugged, trying for nonchalance when she couldn't deny the pleasure of knowing he'd been out there. "Probably."

"By all means, invite him in for breakfast." Myrtle bustled back to the kitchen.

A nervous ripple shook Kate as she went out the door.

He was just doing his job, she told herself. He wasn't looking out for her because he cared and she was only offering because it was the polite thing to do. Plus, Myrtle had insisted. The crisp morning air cooled her skin through her twill pants and lightweight cotton sweater.

Brody rolled down his window as she approached the car. He wore his uniform beneath his jacket and a thermos sat on the seat next to him.

"Care to come in for breakfast?" she asked.

Surprise flared in his eyes before a slow smile spread across his face. "Love to."

Feeling awkward because of the rush of warmth his smile generated in her, she sternly reminded herself this wasn't some sort of date. She stepped back when he opened the door. He moved slowly, stiffly from the car. White lines appeared around his compressed mouth. Concern and guilt coursed through her because he'd spent an uncomfortable night sitting in his car while she peacefully slept.

"After you," he said with a sweeping gesture of his hand. They walked to the house with her slightly ahead of him and, as they stepped onto the sidewalk leading to Myrtle's door, she glanced back. Was he limping? He met her gaze with raised brows and walked past her without a limp. Must have been her imagination.

In the time it took Kate to bring the sheriff in, Myrtle had set the dining-room table for three. In the middle of the table sat the plate of bacon and the warming dish full of scrambled eggs.

Myrtle came out of the kitchen carrying a pitcher of

orange juice. "Sheriff McClain. What a pleasant surprise," she gushed, her obvious affection for him glow-
ing in her eyes. "Have a seat, you two."

"Kate." Brody held out a chair and once she was
settled, he held out a chair for Myrtle. Kate liked and
appreciated Brody's good manners. Paul had never been
so solicitous.

It felt strange sharing a table, a meal with Brody. It
was as if they were friends or something. She couldn't
deny she was grateful for his presence, even if he was
there only because he was doing his job. He made her
feel safe and cared for.

They ate and talked and Kate enjoyed herself.
Because of Myrtle's presence, the conversation never
strayed to Paul or his death. For a short time, Kate was
able to put all the bad stuff that had happened over the
past weeks aside. They talked about everything from
movies to politics to sports.

Kate was amused to discover that she and Brody
shared similar tastes. She only wished they had similar agendas. His was to protect her, yes, but she suspected he wanted to make sure she truly was innocent
of any wrongdoing in order to protect his town. She
wanted answers that would prove her innocence, but
mostly to give her peace so she could move on with
her life.

As they cleared the plates, Myrtle paused and addressed Brody, "Sheriff, Kate and I are headed to church
now. Would you care to join us?"

Brody blinked. He hadn't been to church in years.
Not since he was old enough to refuse while his mother

and siblings still attended. The void inside of him seemed magnified in church. "I…"

Kate laid a warm hand on his arm. "You don't have to go. Myrtle and I will be fine."

He frowned. He didn't like the idea of her going somewhere unattended. He'd go and hang out in front. Just in case those men tried anything. "I'll come with you."

Kate's pleased smile slid through him with surprising ease, making him feel good. As he followed the ladies out of the house and headed toward the little white chapel in the middle of town, he chastised himself for liking how good her pleasure made him feel.

He wasn't out to win her over. His job was to protect her and his town. He couldn't ever forget the job was what mattered. He'd forgotten that important rule once and wasn't about to do it again.

They approached the wide-open doors of the church. Many of the townsfolk milled around the door, chatting, greeting each other before filing inside. Brody took it all in with a jaundiced eye. He didn't see the point. Hadn't seen the point in worship or church for a long time. Not when God had deserted him when he'd required Him most.

Brody stopped on the top stair and moved off to the side.

"You're not coming in?" Kate asked as she stepped to the side with him. She had a Bible she'd brought from Myrtle's securely held in one hand.

"No. I'll wait out here for you." He folded his arms across his chest. He found himself studying the way the sunlight glinted in Kate's copper-colored hair, making some of the strands appear almost gold in tone.

"Suit yourself," she said, but she didn't move away as he expected her to.

"Well, hello, Sheriff."

Brody turned toward the gruff male voice. Mr. Leighton, the great-grandson of the town's founding father, hobbled his eighty-plus-years frame up the stairs. "Mr. Leighton. How are you today?"

"Better now that I see you've decided to join us this morning." The older man's dark blue eyes peered at Kate. "Who's she?"

"Mr. Leighton, this is Kate Wheeler. She's in town for…a while."

Mr. Leighton held out his bony hand to Kate. She shook it. "Hello, Mr. Leighton. It's a pleasure to meet you."

"The pleasure is mine, dear." He released her hand and shifted his gaze back to Brody. "Well, escort the lady in, young man."

"I'm not coming in," Brody said quickly. "The town's better served if I stay on duty."

Mr. Leighton adjusted his paisley tie. "You're here so there must be a deputy holding down the fort." Mr. Leighton raised a white brow. "Correct?"

Brody frowned, feeling caught in a trap of his own making. "Yes, but I…" He paused when he noticed the amused and challenging gleam in Kate's green eyes. Without a word spoken she asserted more pressure on him than Leighton's direct offense.

His gaze darted between the two. He decided he could tolerate one hour spent inside the church for the good of Havensport's sheriff's department. He didn't want to offend the department's number-one supporting family. "Shall we?"

"Let's," she said cheerily and she took his arm.

Not missing Mr. Leighton's approving smile, Brody escorted Kate inside and through the double doors leading to the sanctuary. The dark, oak walls of the chapel could have been oppressive if not for the large windows on either side of the building that allowed sunlight to stream in.

As they moved down the center aisle between rows of wooden pews, a feeling stole over Brody. It wasn't what he expected. There was no anger or hurt. No gaping void. He didn't feel out of place. He didn't feel unwelcome. Searching inside himself, he tried to decipher what it was he felt.

They took seats in the third row next to Myrtle. Brody nodded in greeting to several familiar faces. He saw Mrs. Kim, one of the elementary school teachers, and her family; Dora Able, who owned the bookstore in town; Deputy Teal and his family. Which meant that Deputy Anderson was on duty.

Kate leaned in close to whisper. "If you're uncomfortable, you can leave. You don't have to be here."

"I'm not uncomfortable."

"Well, that's sure a fierce scowl on your face," she whispered again.

Deliberately relaxing his features, he whispered back. "I want to be here."

And he realized he did. The feeling that he couldn't identify was belonging. He belonged among these people. This was his town. He settled back, enjoying the insight. He'd always felt protective of Havensport but not really connected. A smile tugged at his mouth. He had connected with the people here. They looked to him to keep them safe.

A man rose and went to the pulpit. Brody had met Pastor Sims a few times. The man was average in height, medium build with light eyes and dark hair. Brody had found the pastor engaging on the few occasions they'd crossed paths.

Pastor Sims asked the congregation to open their hymnals. Kate leaned forward to take one from the pocket attached to the back of the pew in front of them. Her graceful fingers leafed through the pages until she came to the opening hymn. Organ music coming from the loft at the back of the chapel filled the air.

Brody recognized the melody and a glance at the book in Kate's hands confirmed it. As voices joined the organ music, the words to the hymn bubbled inside Brody from some long-forgotten place. He clamped his jaw shut.

But the pressure building in his chest physically hurt. He tried to concentrate on anything other than the growing urgency to unite his voice in worship with the others in the sanctuary. On the second refrain he couldn't hold out any longer. The words tumbled out, at first low and weak but gaining in volume and boldness.

As he sang he felt lighter, the pain in his chest receded, leaving him vaguely dizzy.

The song ended and then another began. Again the

words came easily. Brody felt Kate's warm gaze, but he couldn't acknowledge her curiosity. This desire to communicate with God was too new, too unexpected. And he wasn't sure how to take his sudden ache to worship.

Later, after several more songs and after the congregation had put away their hymnals, Brody crossed his arms over his chest in defense against anything the pastor might say about God.

"If you have your Bibles, please turn to second Corinthians, chapter twelve, verse nine," Pastor Sims instructed.

Brody watched Kate deftly turn to the page in her Bible as if she knew exactly where that passage was without having to think about it. She scooted the Bible closer so he could see it better. Though he appreciated her thoughtfulness, he had no intention of looking.

As the pastor began to speak, Brody let his mind wander to Kate's situation. Again he wondered just how involved she was in her husband's death. And what she wasn't telling him.

His mind tangled on something the pastor said. And without consciously deciding, Brody found himself listening.

"The Lord said to Paul, 'My grace is sufficient for you, for My strength is made perfect in weakness.' It's important to realize that the Lord's answer to Paul wasn't punitive. Rather, it affirms that no matter what befalls us, be it a sickness, a loss of a job or the death of a loved one, that Jesus' grace can sustain us if we choose to allow Him into our lives."

What was this grace the pastor was talking about? Brody grappled to understand.

And, as if Pastor Sims had a direct connection into his thoughts, he said, "Grace is God's undeserved favor that can bring us healing, both physical and emotional. God's grace can protect us, guide us. In our deepest pain, deepest weakness, God's goodness and faithfulness are revealed."

The pastor went on to give examples from various Bible passages. He spoke of Noah. Of Jacob and Joseph. David and Paul.

And Brody sat there in the third row feeling as if God was talking directly to him. He felt that he was on the brink of…he didn't know what.

Something inside him wanted to respond, wanted to seek this favor, this grace the pastor spoke of. Brody wanted God's strength.

But the questions rose. Why did his father have to die? Why hadn't God protected his father? Why hadn't God protected Brody? The clamoring in his head drowned out the rest of what the pastor had to say.

When the time came for the pastor's prayer, Brody's gaze wandered over the people with their bowed heads and closed eyes. Did they really believe their prayers would make a difference?

His gaze rested on Kate. Her lips moved with silent words. Could a woman who'd killed her husband sit in church and pray like that? Could she find absolution when he couldn't even find God?

Focus on the job, boyo. Time would tell him of Kate's innocence or guilt.

Soon they were filing out with the rest of the Havensport's townspeople. Brody shook hands with several people, ruffled the hair of a toddler and found that sense of belonging firmly taking up residence in his heart.

He and Kate walked Myrtle back to her home and then taking his cruiser, headed first to the mercantile to collect more boxes and then to the Kinsey house.

Brody was thankful Kate didn't ask any questions about his thoughts on the church service or the pastor's sermon. He wasn't prepared to delve into what he was feeling or thinking about God and grace and unanswered questions.

He doubted he'd ever be.

The boxes she'd had delivered the day before were stacked near the front door. Brody had also had the lock on the front door fixed. Kate liked his thoroughness. They went inside and Kate was overwhelmed with the task at hand.

"You know, you could call the local donation center. I'm sure they'd have people willing to come take care of this," Brody suggested, his tone gentle as if he could sense her reluctance to dive right in.

"That's a good idea. I'll do that with the furniture and stuff. But I want to go through his personal items. Maybe I'll find some closure. Something."

They worked together as a team. Brody would dump the contents of drawers into a box and she'd sift through the items, looking for something to tell her who Paul really was and why he'd been killed.

Several hours later, with nothing significant to show for their efforts, Kate's head pounded with frustration. They'd gone through every drawer and bedroom closet.

They'd stripped the beds, emptied the linen closet and looked through the toiletries in the bathroom. Brody had stacked the now-full boxes in a corner of the living room and was dragging stuff out of the entryway closet.

She pulled an empty box closer. Rubber boots, a duffel bag full of tennis gear, an empty briefcase. Brody handed her the coats. She searched the pockets of each as she had every other piece of clothing in the house. From the inside pocket of a black leather jacket, sharp edges of paper poked at her hand. Her heart rate accelerated. She tugged out the folded envelope.

She ran her fingertip along the edge of the envelope. It had already been opened. She pulled out the sheets of paper. Letters. Only letters. She released the air trapped in her lungs and breathed in a sickly, sweet scent of perfume. She looked closer. The words were written in a flowing handwriting and in a language she didn't recognize.

"Kate? You okay?"

She glanced up to meet Brody's concerned gaze. "This isn't in English." She held up her find.

He moved to her side. She handed him the bundle and watched as his big capable hands shuffled through the pages. "Looks Cyrillic."

Her brows rose. "What?"

"Russian."

"How do you know?" she asked.

"One of the locals, Mr. Waskasky, is from St. Petersburg. He used to teach Russian studies at the university. I've seen writing like this in his house. He'll be able to translate these."

Russian. She shivered. Who was this man she'd been married to for four years? The doubts, the questions and insecurities swelled and bubbled, buffeting her like the crashing surf outside. Once again she was reminded that the only way she'd find any measure of peace was to find the truth.

"Can we go see him now?" she asked Brody.

Brody took her hand, his grip strong and reassuring. Warmth suffused her arm and chased away her chills. She wanted to hang on to that warmth, that anchor, but she let go and moved toward the door ahead of him.

Though she was thankful that at the moment he was dedicated to helping her, she couldn't allow herself to depend on him in the long run, no matter how much her heart wanted her to. She couldn't forget that he was a man dedicated to a dangerous career. They could never have a future together.

Mr. Waskasky wasn't home when they went by his condo in a newer development at the edge of town. Brody left his card with a note, asking for the older man to call him when he returned.

Disappointment showed bright in Kate's green eyes but she didn't say much as Brody drove her back to Myrtle's.

They were walking into the small house when the radio attached to his shoulder crackled and hissed. Teal's voice came through. "Sheriff, we've got a situation at the high school."

Brody reached up and pressed the respond button. "Serious?"

"No. But the principal wants you there."

"Copy that. On my way."

He met Kate's wide-eyed stare.

"You're leaving?"

"I have a job to do."

Myrtle laid a hand on her arm. "You'll be fine here, dear."

Kate gave her a wan smile before turning back to Brody. He narrowed his gaze at the slight pallor of her complexion.

"I'll be back," he offered.

She nodded, her expression bleak and vulnerable. Something in Brody shifted, softened, making him want to take her hand again and reassure her. Making him think of the way he'd almost kissed her less than forty-eight hours ago. He forced himself to remember his resolve to remain unaffected by her act.

He couldn't risk paying more for believing in her. She was a job. He wouldn't let it get personal. He turned to go.

"The letters!" Kate thrust the sheets of paper toward him.

"Right." Caution warned she could be setting him up with her false trust. He reached for the papers. "I'll drop them off with Mr. Waskasky when I'm done. He should be home by then."

She didn't let go. "I'm going with you."

"You can't."

"I'm going with you," she repeated, her expression determined.

"Kate—"

"What if you don't come back?"

Reacting to the urgency and desperation in her tone, Brody sought to reassure her. "This is a routine incident. I'll be back. Then we can go see about the letter together."

Her gaze searched his face as if she were deciding whether to trust him or not. Finally, she gave a short nod. "Fine."

Brody left, shutting the door firmly behind him. As he heard the click of the lock slide into place he couldn't shake the unsettled feeling that no matter how much he tried to protect himself, he was still vulnerable to a red-haired woman with worry in her wide green eyes.

EIGHT

Kate gathered up the remains of the clam chowder dinner she'd shared with Myrtle and headed into the kitchen. Though she enjoyed Myrtle's company, she couldn't shake a restless disappointment. Her life hadn't turned out the way she'd planned. She'd so wanted a normal, all-American life. How had she ended up with so much deceit?

Myrtle smiled as she entered. "Thank you, dear. Just put those dishes on the counter. I'll take care of them later."

"I'll wash them. It's the least I can do for all your kindness." Kate went to the sink. Nervous energy made her edgy and she needed something to do. She glanced at the old wooden cuckoo clock hanging on the pale yellow wall of the kitchen.

Three hours. Where was Brody?

Kate washed the dinner dishes, her hands working automatically, scrubbing and wiping. The simple task left her mind to wander.

Trouble at the high school. Teenagers with too much time on their hands was Myrtle's guess.

But what if it was something more? What if Brody was hurt and didn't return? An ache tightened in her chest. She recognized the sensation. Only this time it was more acute.

She scrubbed harder at the soup bowl in her hand. She didn't want to like Brody, much less worry about him. But the ache, full of anxiety, fear and dread was the same she'd experienced every time her father went off on one of his missions.

As a child, she hadn't understood why her mother was so anxious every time her father left. Sometimes he disappeared in the middle of the night. Her mother would lock herself away in her room and cry, leaving Kate alone and confused.

It wasn't until Kate was nine and her father was hurt, a wound in the shoulder from an explosive of some sort, that she'd begun to grasp the nature of his job. And though Brody wasn't a covert operations specialist like her father, he was a cop. And a cop's life was as iffy and dangerous. Anything could happen.

What if he didn't come back? The question played like a broken record in her mind and an invisible band across her chest squeezed tighter. She was only concerned because he had the letter, concerned that he'd have it translated without her. She picked up a dish towel and dried a blue plate.

No. He'd said he'd wait, that she could go with him. But could she trust him to keep his word? He hadn't given her any reason not to, but Paul's whispered warning not to trust anyone lurked in her mind.

She scoffed out loud. Hadn't Paul proven he was the one not to be trusted? He'd lived a double life, lied to her and endangered her. No, she wouldn't compare Brody to Paul.

"Did you say something, dear?" Myrtle asked as she tidied the counters.

"I was wondering where Sheriff McClain was."

"Oh, I'm sure he'll return soon."

Kate nodded and stacked the dishes to the side.

"Thank you for helping." Myrtle put the clean dishes in the cupboards.

Kate leaned against the sink. "Thank you for your wonderful hospitality."

"I must confess it's good to have company. My late husband, Fred, used to say I lived to entertain, but it's been years since I had a guest."

"How long ago did your husband die?"

"Fred passed on about ten years ago now. He was a good man." Myrtle stared off into memories. "So full of life. He found humor in everything and he made our years together blissful. He was my soul mate, created by God to love me and me him."

Touched by the sentiment, Kate wondered if she'd ever find that kind of bliss, find her soul mate, the one created by God for her. She doubted it. She'd never risk her heart again.

Looking back, she knew bliss hadn't been there with Paul. He'd been safe, steady, which was what she'd wanted. What she still wanted, but she knew better now. Paul hadn't come close to giving her the security she craved. She couldn't imagine loving someone so deeply that you knew they were a gift from above.

An image of Brody rose in her mind. His dark

probing eyes, his strong jaw and his mouth with its devastating grin. Would his kiss be as devastating?

Whoa! Kate shook her head to clear her mind. Not what she should be thinking about. Instead, she thought about how he made her feel so safe and cared for. He really listened. He never talked over her the way Paul had. The sheriff was a gentleman. But she had no intention of becoming his lady.

Myrtle's gaze pinned her to the counter, as if she could see into her heart, laying bare her doubts.

"To completely love another person is to experience the essence of God."

Myrtle's words seeped deep into Kate's soul. "I doubt I'll find that kind of love."

"Love isn't something that can be planned or scheduled. Love is a choice."

"Love is full of risks," Kate countered.

Myrtle laughed softly. "Life would be boring without risks."

Growing uncomfortable with the direction of the conversation, Kate broke eye contact to glance once again at the clock. She hated this waiting and wondering and worrying. She could never, ever be a police officer's wife.

"Would you care for some tea, dear?" Myrtle asked.

With a sigh, Kate resigned herself to waiting. "That would be lovely, thank you." She walked to the French doors leading to the wooden deck. "I'm going to step out for some fresh air."

"Good idea. After the last few days you've had, with those nasty men trying to grab you, you need a little rest and relaxation."

She gave Myrtle a half smile. Myrtle had questioned her during their meal and Kate had given her as vaguely truthful answers as she could. She didn't want to worry the kind older woman. She didn't want anybody else to be drawn into this mess.

She stepped out onto the deck. A slight breeze ruffled through her hair and sent a chill down her spine.

The sound of the surf drew her attention to the path that led between the shrubs surrounding the yard. She longed to walk down to the water's edge, to feel the soothing sand beneath her feet.

Instead she wrapped her arms around her middle and leaned against the railing. On the horizon, the blue-green water met the soft pinks and oranges of the setting sun like a watercolor canvas, serene and lovely.

Her mind turned to the problem at hand. She had to make plans in case the sheriff didn't return. She swallowed against the panic that thought brought. She needed to be logical, practical. She couldn't rely on anyone else.

If she didn't get the letters back, then she'd head to New York state. She'd memorized the return address: 425 W 5th, Brighton Beach, New York. She hoped she'd find the answers to her questions there.

And if Brody did return?

She had a feeling he wouldn't leave her to do this alone. And she didn't know how she felt about that.

A whisper of movement came from the bushes to her right. Her throat constricted and terror reared up with lightning speed. She whirled around.

A seagull stared at her through the green leaves of the bush.

She laughed at her own paranoia. She was safe on Myrtle's deck.

She'd turned to go back in when a movement in her peripheral vision alerted her seconds before a hand clamped harshly over her mouth. She grabbed at the arms that dragged her across the deck, down the stairs and through the bushes.

Dear God, please save me!

Where was Brody?

Brody pulled his cruiser up to the curb behind Warren's vehicle and threw the gearshift into Park. The trouble at the school had taken longer than he'd anticipated. A group of teens, some local, a few out-of-towners, had broken in and vandalized the halls. Brody had to track down each kid's parents and then he'd stuck around to supervise the cleaning that the principal had demanded the kids do rather than pressing charges.

It was growing late, and he knew Kate would be disappointed when he told her he'd heard from Mr. Waskasky, who wouldn't be able to help until the morning.

Brody got out of the car and walked toward Warren's car. He frowned. Warren wasn't in the driver's seat. His gaze narrowed on the cottage. Warren was going to get an earful. He'd told the young deputy to stay outside, not to make his presence a bother by bugging the ladies.

He charged up the stairs and knocked on the door. A moment later Myrtle answered.

"Sheriff, you're back." She waved him in. "I was just getting tea and a cake ready to take out to Kate."

"Where's Deputy Teal?" he asked.

"I haven't seen Warren this evening." Myrtle looked over his shoulder and frowned. "I hadn't noticed his car."

His senses went on the alert. "Where's Kate?"

"On the deck out back."

He palmed the radio attached to his shoulder and radioed the station.

"Anderson, here."

"Have you heard from Warren?"

"No, not since he left this afternoon."

Brody clenched his fist. "Come to Myrtle Kirby's. I need your help."

"Should I call Sheriff Talbot?"

"No," Brody barked, irritated that the older deputy would automatically suggest calling his old boss. He wasn't going to call in the retired sheriff. It was bad enough that Warren had gone missing. He didn't need to add to the questions and scrutiny that would come from Sheriff Talbot. "Just get here."

He clicked off the radio. He'd started back down the stairs when he heard a low moan coming from under the porch. Brody found Warren facedown in the dirt, blood, still sticky and wet, smeared on the back of his head.

Brody dragged him out. "What happened?"

Warren blinked and struggled to sit up. "Two men. I got out, they asked for directions. One hit me from behind."

Greg Anderson's car screeched to a halt behind Brody's car. People emerged from neighboring houses, obviously curious about the police cars in front of Myrtle's.

Brody and Greg helped Warren to a chair on the porch.

"Oh, my," exclaimed Myrtle when she saw the state of the deputy. She turned her troubled gaze on Brody. "Kate?"

Brody left Warren to Greg's care and stormed around the house to the back deck. Empty. Dread gripped his gut.

Myrtle stepped out from the house. "She was here just a bit ago. Maybe she went down to the beach." The worry in her voice was unmistakable.

Brody gritted his teeth and charged across the grass. He skidded to halt when he came to one of Kate's shoes lying near the bushes. He cursed as terror slammed into his chest. He'd failed to protect her.

Or she'd gone of her own free will.

In which case, he'd failed to do his job. Again.

"I'll find her." He was determined to figure her out. And when he did he'd send her back to Los Angeles, back to be someone else's problem.

He moved more cautiously toward the path leading through the bushes to the beach. His heart rate picked up speed when his gaze snagged on the telltale signs of a struggle where the grass met the sand. Large indentations—like those of men's boots—marred the sand and deep grooves—like that of someone being dragged— ran down the path and around the bushes.

Dread seized him. He *had* failed her. His hand

reached for his sidearm as he emerged from the path onto the beach. His gaze swung about, searching the growing darkness. The beach was empty.

She could be anywhere by now. To the right, the bushes gave way to the backyard of Myrtle's neighbor and to the left, the bushes ended at drainpipes that dumped the town's rainwater, creating a rocky inlet. Logic and gut instinct told him to go left.

He ran toward the drainpipes. He skidded to a halt as a figure stumbled out from behind the bushes.

"Kate!"

In her hand she held a big stick. Her clothes were wet and dirty. Her eyes widened, and then she went down in a heap at his feet. His breath froze and he dropped to his knees.

Flashes of his father's lifeless body threatened to cripple him. He forced himself to stay focused on Kate. In the waning light he saw the ugly gash at her temple and the bruises on her face.

"Kate, Kate!"

She didn't wake.

Strangling with panic, Brody fought back the fear gripping him and did something he hadn't done since he was ten years old.

"Lord, please don't let her die."

Kate struggled from the drifting, floating sensation that held her body and her mind. Her eyelids fluttered open. Dull light stung her eyes and she blinked.

Where was she?

Sterile walls, a firm mattress, the hanging bag of

fluid with a tube running down to a shunt stuck into her right hand. A hospital.

Aches on various parts of her body made themselves known with dull intensity. She closed her eyes again, trying to sink back to the sweet ignorance of slumber, but the images flicking through her mind like a projector on high speed wouldn't allow her ease.

Instead, fear built within her chest as she remembered the hands around her. Terror clawed at her throat, cutting off her air as she replayed being dragged away from the shelter of Myrtle's house. She fought to breathe, her body thrashed as she tried to sit up, to run.

Pain exploded in her head causing bright light to blot out her vision. She gritted her teeth. She had to leave. She wasn't safe.

Suddenly, strong hands pushed her back into the pillows. Fresh panic swelled. The restraints holding her down were too strong. She couldn't break free. "No."

"Shhhh, Kate. You're safe."

She recognized the voice. She stilled. "Brody?"

The hands holding her down gentled to a calming caress. "Yes. I'm here."

Slowly, she opened her eyes to assure herself he was real. His face came into focus, and relief cascaded swiftly through her like an early-spring waterfall, powerful and refreshing.

She sighed and drifted as the tension eased from her body. Her head throbbed as adrenaline left to be replaced by oxygen.

She wasn't sure what to make of Brody's presence.

The thudding of her heart took on a different beat, less frantic but just as wild. She felt safe, yet threatened. Comforted, yet panicked. And none of it had anything to do with her situation and everything to do with the man beside the bed.

She didn't want to need him, she shouldn't want to rely on him. Even so, she was thankful he was there. And she knew in her soul that he was the reason she was still alive.

God had answered her prayers by providing her with a protector here on earth, though Brody wouldn't appreciate that title. A smile played at the corners of her mouth. A spasm of pain radiated through her head for her effort. She closed her eyes, letting the ache wash over her and ebb away as the smile fell.

There was still so much to do and so many questions that needed to be answered. And as much as she hated to admit it, she couldn't chase down the answers on her own. She needed Brody, needed his strength, his intelligence and his protection. She needed him to trust her. But she had to keep her heart safe. She couldn't allow herself to fall for him. He was the opposite of the stable, secure life she longed for.

But for now she could use his help.

Her gaze sought him. He'd taken a seat next to the bed. He no longer wore his brown uniform; instead, a light blue button-down shirt and faded jeans hugged his big body. Lines of tension framed his ebony eyes. His clean-shaven cheeks emphasized his hard jaw.

"Hi." The word came out as a croak.

Brody immediately moved to pour her a cup of

water. Gently he held the cup to her bruised and swollen lips. The water hit her mouth, cool and flowing. She greedily drank, relieving the parchedness of her throat. When the cup was drained, he sat.

"Better?"

"Much." She tried not to wince. Talking stung her lips and her jaw was sore. She ran her tongue around her mouth, noting thankfully that she wasn't missing any teeth. "How did I get here?"

"I found you unconscious on the beach."

He definitely was sent by God. "You saved my life. Thank you."

"If I'd have been doing my job better, you wouldn't have been in that situation."

His tone of self-recrimination pulled at her heart. She reached for his hand. He enfolded hers in his capable fingers, the pressure reassuring and thrilling. "You couldn't have known they'd be so bold as to take me from Myrtle's deck."

"What happened?"

She took a deep breath and strove for logical, unemotional. "I was grabbed from behind and dragged down the beach. I struggled, one of them hit me. I went down hard. I managed to grab a piece of driftwood. I got a few good hits in. They must have heard you coming because all of a sudden they left." She ran her tongue over the tender lump in her lip.

"Did they say anything?"

Gaining his trust needed to start now. It was her move. If she expected him to continue to help her and protect her, she need to be honest with him and put some trust in him, as well. "They kept asking me where the disk was."

Two little grooves appeared between his eyes as his brows lowered. "A disk?" His demeanor shifted, becoming remote, distant. Coplike. "Tell me about the disk."

She swallowed, hating the suspicion in his dark gaze. "I don't know anything."

"Where's the disk, Kate?"

"I don't know."

"Then why do they think you have it?"

"I... When I found Paul, he was still alive. He asked for Gordon, our lawyer and then he...before he died in my arms, he said, 'I told them you have it.' He didn't tell me what 'it' was."

Brody stared at her for a long, taut moment. His eyes searched her face, peeling away the layers of her heart, looking for hidden secrets. She wanted to lift her chin and dare him to disbelieve her.

Instead she allowed herself to be laid bare and vulnerable beneath his steel-eyed gaze. She didn't have any secrets. Not now. What he saw was what he got.

"Will you help me find that disk, Brody?" she asked, her voice a notch above a whisper. It was so hard to ask for help. But she needed it. She needed him. She tensed, waiting, hoping for his answer of yes.

His gaze came to rest on her battered lip, his expression softened ever so slightly before he spoke. "Yes, I'll help you."

A stone of worry lifted from around her neck. Fatigue overwhelmed her. She sank back and melted into the bed.

"But I need a promise from you, Kate."

She stiffened, wary. "What?"

"From now on you have to be completely honest with me."

"Of course," she answered quickly and a bit sheepishly. "Before, I...I didn't know if I could trust you."

"And now?"

She swallowed. For all his gruff and bluster, she sensed a good man lurked deep inside. She jumped in with both feet and prayed for a soft landing. "I trust you. God sent me the guardian angel I prayed for and you're it."

NINE

"**I**'m no angel," Brody scoffed.

"I said you're my guardian angel, as in protector. Not that you're angelic."

Her humor sliced through him. She still had spunk. He liked that. Admired it, too. "There's a difference?"

"Hmmm, angelic equals perfect and heavenly."

His mouth quirked to one side. "Perfect, I'm not."

"No, you're very human," she agreed, with a smile in her voice. "The only real angels I know of are in the Bible." Her eyelids fluttered. She was losing it, but trying so hard not to give in.

Then she focused her gaze and the undisguised trust in her eyes caught him off guard. No one but his sister had ever looked at him like that.

But his reaction to Kate was far from brotherly.

He wanted to take her into his arms and soothe away the hurt she'd suffered. He wanted to run his fingers through her red curls and feel the texture slide against his skin, he wanted to fill his lungs with her sweet scent and lose himself in her embrace. He wanted to shield her from the world.

But none of those things were possible.

Instead, he focused on her battered face, on the bandage over the gash at her temple. He hated seeing her so bruised and vulnerable. He wanted to beat something, someone to a pulp. He'd failed to protect her. It wouldn't happen again.

"You're flawed in a good way," she said.

Her words stung. How could Kate see his flaws as good? With Elise, he'd had a major lapse in judgment, had allowed his emotions to rule his actions. And he'd paid the price. His career effectively snuffed out, his ego shredded and his body left damaged. There was nothing good about any of his past.

"Kate, I don't know what you think you know…" he trailed off as her eyes closed and she sighed.

"I know you're here and that's all that matters." Her words were slurred as the fatigue she'd been fighting overcame her.

His heart twisted in his chest. He didn't deserve her trust. He couldn't live up to her expectations. He should call the Feds and let them deal with the situation.

Her eyes opened, panic shining in the emerald depths. "No. You promised you'd help me."

He hadn't realized he'd spoken his last thought out loud. "Kate, the Feds are better equipped to protect you."

"Please, no one else."

Her plea was an arrow to his heart. And a reminder of what happened before. "Rest, Kate. We'll talk about this when you're stronger."

"The letters?"

"Safe. I'll ask Mr. Waskasky to come here to translate them tomorrow."

She relaxed. "Thank you."

"Did Paul give you any strange keys or anything out of the ordinary?"

She thought for a moment. "No. The last thing he'd given me was a birthday present a year and half ago."

"And that was?"

She gave a small wry laugh. "My very practical, very useful purse." She glanced around. "I suppose it's still at Myrtle's."

"I'll have it brought over."

"I'd appreciate it. A lady feels naked without her purse."

Brody blinked and tried to banish the image her words conjured up. He smoothed a curl behind her ear, his knuckle grazed her cheek. Her skin was soft, her hair silky. His stomach muscles clenched. She didn't deserve this pain. "Rest now, okay?"

"Hmmm." Her eyes closed as she nuzzled against his hand. "You'll stay?"

Tenderness bloomed, tightening his chest. He leaned in and kissed her forehead. "Yes, I'll stay."

Saying those words were like hitting the rewind button on his life. He'd promised Elise he'd help her, too. And the result had been disastrous.

Kate made a soft little sound deep in her throat. Then her breathing became even and rhythmic. Watching her sleep, Brody released the tension he'd held since he'd found her on the beach.

His gut-level instincts told him she was telling the truth when she said she didn't know anything about the disk. Which left them with another uncovered piece of the puzzle as to why she was in danger.

The situation was becoming more complicated by the minute. And his attraction to Kate was only making matters worse. He had to get a grip. He knew from experience he couldn't protect Kate and care about her at the same time. In doing so he compromised his judgment and jeopardized his focus.

Keep your mind on the job.

His father's motto slapped him upside the head. He wished he'd listened last time. This time he would.

He had a tough decision to make. Helping Kate meant leaving the town unprotected. That was unacceptable. He didn't take his pledge to protect and serve the community of Havensport lightly. He knew what he had to do—call old Sheriff Talbot. The one person in Havensport who knew the truth. The one person who would demand to know why Brody needed to do this.

And the answer had Brody tied up in knots.

Kate awoke to voices in her head.

She had no way to distinguish time, no way to know if she'd slept for a moment or for hours. Turning her head, she listened. Brody's distinct, velvet-coated tones sent waves of comfort over her, and then another voice. A burly, masculine sound that stole her calmness away. She lay still, tense. The two men spoke at a hushed level, but she made out the words. Was the other man Brody's father?

"How long do you need?"

"Don't know." Brody's voice suggested the shrug Kate could envision.

"This is way too risky. Let the Feds handle her."

Kate nearly bolted upright in protest, but Brody's quick response soothed her panic.

"I gave her my word."

"Why are you doing this to yourself again?"

"Look, Sheriff—"

"No, you look, *Sheriff*. I'm no longer sheriff here, you are. You have a responsibility to this town."

Kate stifled a groan. She hadn't realized she was jeopardizing Brody's job by asking for his help. But what was she to do? She wished she had the courage to handle this alone. But she didn't. She needed Brody. Needed his protection.

"I'm entitled to a vacation after three years without."

A long silent moment stretched taut through the hospital room.

Kate wanted to open her eyes. She wanted to see the two men, but they might notice she was awake and halt their conversation. She had to know what helping her would cost Brody. Though how she'd ever repay him, she didn't know.

"A vacation then," the other man said with grudging reluctance.

"Effective immediately."

"Son, I just don't want you to get hurt again."

Kate noted the paternal caring to the other man's tone and wondered what he meant by his words. How had

Get 2 Books FREE!

Steeple Hill Books,
publisher of inspirational fiction, presents

Love Inspired
SUSPENSE

A SERIES OF EDGE-OF-YOUR-SEAT SUSPENSE NOVELS

FREE BOOKS!
Get two free books by acclaimed, inspirational authors!

FREE GIFTS!
Get two exciting surprise gifts absolutely free!

2 FREE BOOKS

▲ To get your 2 free books and 2 free gifts, affix this peel-off sticker to the reply card and mail it today!

We'd like to send you two free books to introduce you to the *Love Inspired® Suspense* series. Your two books have a combined cover price of $9.98 in the U.S. and $11.98 in Canada, but they are yours free! We'll even send you two wonderful surprise gifts. You can't lose!

GET 2 FREE BOOKS!

HURRY!
Return this card promptly to get **2 FREE Books** *and* **2 FREE** *Bonus Gifts!*

Love Inspired.
SUSPENSE

YES! *Please send me the 2 FREE Love Inspired® Suspense books and 2 FREE gifts for which I qualify. I understand that I am under no obligation to purchase anything further, as explained on the back of this card.*

affix
free
books
sticker
here

323 IDL EL4Z   **123 IDL EL3Z**

FIRST NAME	LAST NAME

ADDRESS

APT.#	CITY

STATE/PROV.	ZIP/POSTAL CODE

Steeple
Hill®

Steeple Hill Reader Service®—Here's How It Works:

Accepting your 2 free books and 2 free gifts places you under no obligation to buy anything. You may keep the books and gifts and return the shipping statement marked "cancel." If you do not cancel, about a month later we will send you 4 additional books and bill you just $3.99 each in the U.S. or $4.74 each in Canada, plus 25¢ shipping & handling per book and applicable taxes if any.* That's the complete price, and — compared to cover prices of $4.99 each in the U.S. and $5.99 each in Canada — it's quite a bargain! You may cancel at any time, but if you choose to continue, every month we'll send you 4 more books, which you may either purchase at the discount price...or return to us and cancel your subscription.

*Terms and prices subject to change without notice. Sales tax applicable in N.Y. Canadian residents will be charged applicable provincial taxes and GST. All orders subject to approval. Books received may not be as shown. Credit or debit balances in a customer's account(s) may be offset by any other outstanding balance owed by or to the customer. Please allow 4 to 6 weeks for delivery.

If offer card is missing write to: Steeple Hill Reader Service, 3010 Walden Ave., P.O. Box 1867, Buffalo, NY 14240-1867

STEEPLE HILL READER SERVICE
3010 WALDEN AVE
PO BOX 1867
BUFFALO NY 14240-9952

BUSINESS REPLY MAIL
FIRST-CLASS MAIL   PERMIT NO. 717-003   BUFFALO, NY

POSTAGE WILL BE PAID BY ADDRESSEE

NO POSTAGE
NECESSARY
IF MAILED
IN THE
UNITED STATES

Brody been hurt? She realized she knew very little about Brody yet she was putting her life in his hands.

Brody cleared his throat. "I won't."

The swooshing sound of the door opening stopped the conversation.

"Gentlemen. How is our patient?" asked a deep, kindly voice.

Kate took that as her cue to "awaken." She deliberately stirred and slowly opened her eyes. Brody sat beside her bed, his handsome face a welcoming sight, though the strained grooves outlining his smile gave away his tension. Guilt pricked at her conscience. She was using Brody for her own gain.

The doctor stepped forward. Midforties, brown hair, hazel eyes behind horn-rimmed glasses. His expression was friendly yet professional.

A few steps back stood an imposing figure with thick, salt and pepper hair, chiseled features and a grim set to his square jaw. She swallowed as the disapproval in his blue eyes crashed over her like the surf at high tide. She saw little resemblance between Brody and this man. Who was he?

"Kate, the doc wants to examine you and then we can find out how soon you'll be released," Brody said.

She nodded.

"I'll be back in a while. I have some things I must take care of." He covered her fisted hand, his touch reassuring and agonizing.

He'd be back, wouldn't he? She had no choice but to trust in that. She turned her hand in his and gripped his fingers, giving him the reassurance that she'd be okay. With one last squeeze he left, taking her trust and leaving her with hope that he'd keep her safe.

But at what cost?

Later, Kate awoke with a start as the shadows deepened from the afternoon sun spilling through the little rectangular window. There were no voices this time. She was alone.

She found the controls to the bed and raised the back to a sitting position. For a moment the room spun before landing in perfect alignment. She tested her lip. Still painful, less swollen. The doctor had said he wanted to keep her for a few more hours for observation because of her head injury. She had a nasty bump and a slight concussion.

In the quiet of the room she took the opportunity to spend a peaceful moment with God, thanking Him for her rescue, thanking Him for Brody.

The familiar swoosh of the door sounded, then immediately she felt the energy in the room crackle to life as Brody strode in followed by a short, silver-haired man with thick bifocals.

Brody's gaze skimmed over her. "You look good."

Heat flushed her face at his compliment. "Thanks."

She eyed the stranger with curiosity. He was small and round in his brown slacks and tweed coat. His countenance was unassuming and kind.

Brody introduced her visitor. "This is Mr. Waskasky. Do you feel up to listening to the letters?"

The letters. Her heart rate picked up. "Yes."

She steeled herself for the inevitable, for more distressing knowledge about her husband the letters were sure to reveal. For how could perfumed letters, hidden away like love letters, be anything but bad news for the stable, secure life Kate had once thought she had?

She extended her hand. "Hello. Thank you for coming."

The man bustled forward and kissed the back of her hand, his bushy mustache tickling. "My pleasure," he intoned in a heavy accent.

Brody pulled the letters from his pocket. "I waited to have these read until you could hear them."

"I appreciate that," she said. His thoughtfulness and integrity touched her deeply, giving her the courage to hear whatever the letters revealed.

Mr. Waskasky took the envelope and extracted the folded sheets of paper. He cleared his throat. Kate tensed.

"'Petrov, my love, the waiting is killing me. I miss you and can't wait to be with you again. Please, tell me you will come to me before the new year.'"

Each word cut deeper and deeper still. Kate focused her gaze on the textured blanket covering her legs. She wrapped her arms around her middle, trying to hold in the pain, because deep in her gut she knew that Paul was also Petrov.

Page after page of love letters written by a woman named Olga shattered what little remained of Kate's world. Her heart bled until she thought she'd never feel again.

Any love, even the tiniest speck, that she'd held for her dead husband disintegrated. She'd been so blind. Her husband had not *one,* but *two* other identities.

Why had he married her if he had this other woman waiting for him? Who was he really, and what plans had he had for Kate? She felt used, yes, but to what end? Why? Why? The questions spun around her head until she wanted to scream.

Her fingers curled into tight balls. She had to know the answer or she'd never find any peace, never be able to move on with her life.

Brody's big hand closed over her fist. Seeking his steady comfort, she turned her hand until their fingers were entwined. She lifted her gaze to meet his. The compassion evident in his ebony eyes tore at her heart.

Brody's gaze sharply shifted back to Mr. Waskasky. "Read that last part again."

"'You're too naughty, not letting me open the package you sent. Must I wait? My curiosity grows.'"

Kate squeezed Brody's hand. This package could be something. Finally, they had a clue. Brody nodded to her as if he'd heard her thoughts and then quickly thanked Mr. Waskasky before ushering him out.

Brody returned, his expression grim and thoughtful.

She couldn't contain the excitement building inside. "We have to go to New York."

"Yes," he said, his tone distant.

"Brody?"

"Hmmm?"

"Something's bothering you. I can tell."

He rubbed his chin, his fingers rasping against the dark stubble growing along his strong jawline. Kate's gaze followed the movement. She realized with a little start that she was beginning to learn his mannerisms and could sense the shifts in his mood. Their growing closeness was another worry she wasn't sure how to handle.

Finally, he spoke. "Why were the letters left behind?"

She blinked. "What?"

"The letters. We found them pretty easily. If the men who'd broken into the house had found them and could read Cyrillic, they'd know that Pete had sent a package to this woman. Yet, they came after you a second time. If they couldn't read Cyrillic, why'd they leave the letters? This doesn't add up."

Kate gestured wildly with her hands. "*None* of this makes sense. But we can't let this opportunity to find out more go by. We have to leave now."

Brody checked his black-leather-banded watch. "I'll speak with the doc." He strode from the room, his broad shoulders and slim hips moving with a masculine grace that never ceased to impress her.

She picked at the polyester fabric of the blanket as the questions about Paul/Pete/Petrov surfaced again, swirling faster and faster like a whirlpool pulling her under.

"Stop it!" Her voice bounced off the walls and echoed in the sterile room, effectively smoothing out her agitation. She had a goal now. Something to focus her energies toward. Her life depended on finding this woman and the package.

But she had two calls to make.

The first to her boss at the bank, who was more than willing to extend her leave of absence after hearing about her assault. Kate was thankful she hadn't had to reveal the true reason for wanting the extended leave—to unravel the mystery of her husband's death.

The second call was to her lawyer.

"Gordon, it's Kate."

"Kate! I've been calling the house. Where are you?" Gordon Thomas's concerned voice boomed over the telephone wire.

"I'm in the hospital, but I'll be leaving soon."

"Hospital? Are you all right?"

"A little black and blue, but nothing that won't heal."

"Tell me what happened."

"Paul's killers came after me."

"Came after you? How did you know it was them? What did they hope to accomplish?"

"They wanted something I don't have, but I think I know where it is."

"Really? What is it?"

"A computer disk. I don't know what's on it, but I have to find it."

"And you know where it is?"

"Maybe. I'm hoping so."

There was a moment of silence. "Kate, I'm coming out there."

"No, don't." She didn't want to complicate the situation more by having her lawyer show up. Brody might take that as a sign she didn't trust him or worse yet, that she was guilty of something.

"Kate, don't you think it would be better if you had an ally? Someone to help you in this quest? I am your lawyer. I'm on your side. Let me help."

She had help. Brody. He was here and willing. She didn't want to analyze why she preferred Brody over

Gordon. She just did. She tightened her grip on the phone. "Did you know about Pete Kinsey?"

"What is there to know? He was Paul's business partner. You knew that."

Closing her eyes against the hurt of Paul's lies, she stated, "There was no Pete Kinsey."

"Kate, are you sure you're all right? Maybe I should speak with your doctor."

"No! Paul and Pete Kinsey were the same man."

The silence coming from the other end of the line unnerved her. "Gordon? Did you hear me?"

"I heard you, Kate." A note of indulgent sympathy laced his deep gravelly voice. "Come home now. We'll get you some help."

"Help?"

"I know this has been a trying time for you. Guilt can play games with the mind."

Kate raised her brows in shock as the meaning behind Gordon's words sank in. "I have nothing to feel guilty about. Do you think I killed him?"

"Of course not, Kate. Don't be ridiculous."

Kate pinched the bridge of her nose with her free hand. "I am not going crazy and I do not have anything to feel guilt about. Didn't you help Paul with some of his business contracts?"

"Are you questioning my integrity? After all I've done for you and your mother? I assure you I would have told you if I suspected anything inappropriate going on."

Contrition brought tears to her eyes. "I'm sorry. You're right. I know you would. You've been such a --

rock for me my whole life." She wiped at a stray tear. "We found a letter. Gordon, Paul had yet another life."

"What other life?"

"I don't know yet. Does the name Petrov ring any bells?"

"No. Is this person one of Paul's clients?"

She let out a bitter laugh. "Hardly. We're going to New York to see if we can find the disk there."

"We?"

The door to the room swooshed open. Her doctor stepped in followed closely by Brody, pushing a wheelchair.

"I've got to go. I'll call you later." She hung up before Gordon could reply. She met Brody's gaze. "My lawyer," she said quickly to alleviate the wariness in his eyes.

He gave a sharp nod and remained stonily silent as the doctor did a final cursory exam. Satisfied that she was well enough to leave, the doctor signed her discharge papers and left her in Brody's care.

When the second the doctor left, Brody asked, "What did he have to say?"

"He didn't know about Pete or Petrov."

"Did he know anything about the disk?"

"No. He was ready to come here, but I told him not to."

"Why?"

"I think it's better if only you and I go to see this woman. If we show up with a lawyer in tow, she might get spooked."

"You don't think a cop will spook her?" he asked with wry amusement.

"Not if she doesn't know you're a cop."

"Ah." His mouth kicked up on corner. "Undercover it is, then." He walked to the closet. "Myrtle sent some fresh clothing from your suitcase."

Touched by the combined care of Brody and Myrtle, she smiled. "Thank you, Brody, for doing this. I hope it won't cost you too much."

He laid the garments, khakis and an aqua-blue silk blouse on the foot of the bed and gave her a quizzical stare. "Cost me?"

"I overheard you speaking with…your father?"

The corners of Brody's mouth tipped down. "Sheriff Talbot is not my father."

"Oh." Kate blinked. She'd hit a nerve. She opened her mouth to ask, but he was already moving toward the door.

"I'll find a nurse to help you dress, then we'll go find answers about your husband."

She knew the questions she wanted answered, but what questions did Brody have? And would the answers condemn her or absolve her?

TEN

They took an uneventful commuter flight from Hyannis to JFK International Airport. From there they hailed a taxi. Kate sank back into the cab's distressed, red leather seat next to Brody and tried to relax as they traveled down the scenic route along the edge of Jamaica Bay. Anxiety kept her from enjoying the view of sandy beaches, glistening water and strands of trees springing up out of little islands dotting the bay.

She tried not to think too much about what they'd find in Brighton Beach. She hoped this would be the end. And feared that it wouldn't.

The taxi slowed as the traffic became more congested. They inched through various neighborhoods of Brooklyn. Soon they were entering the area known as Little Odessa. She tried to see everything at once yet her heart pounded so loudly in her head it was hard to concentrate and process the interesting sights, so different from those of Los Angeles or the Pacific Northwest where she'd grown up.

"Hey, stop the car," Brody said, his attention riveted on something to his right.

Kate started as the cab abruptly pulled to the side of the street.

"What it is?" She grasped at his sleeve.

Brody pointed out the window to a large, two-story gray concrete warehouse with the words Lanski's Imports emblazoned across the front.

Puzzled, she stared at Brody.

He tugged his wallet from the back pocket of his navy twill pants and pulled out a business card. He flipped it over so she could see the writing. "What's that from?" she asked.

"I found this among Paul's things in the bungalow. Wasn't sure if it meant anything."

Then she remembered.

Brody opened the car door and said to the driver, "Wait. We'll be right back."

A car horn blared and Kate stiffened. The cabby cursed at the black Lincoln Continental waiting impatiently behind them. Another honk. They sure weren't in Havensport anymore. The quaint little town with its friendly and relaxed pace had grown on her in the short amount of time she'd been there.

As Kate slid out of the cab behind Brody and stepped onto the sidewalk, the sun bounced off the pavement and scorched her skin. No cooling summer breeze here.

She followed Brody to the black metal front door of the business. Brody pushed open the door and they stepped in. Men of various builds and ages moved about at a quick pace. Boxes and crates lined the walls. At the other end of the building a large bay door was rolled up. Trucks were being loaded by men driving forklifts burdened by huge crates.

A big burly man with a shaved head and handlebar mustache met them as they moved farther into the work area. He looked impassable in his worn denims and red work shirt straining to contain bulging muscles. "What do you want?"

"I'd like to see the owner," Brody answered, his tone crisp, authoritative.

The man's narrowed gaze raked over them and a chill slithered down Kate's spine. Her senses went on alert. She'd experienced the same type of chill the times she'd thought she was being watched.

"This way," he finally said and walked away.

"Stay close," Brody whispered. "Keep your eyes open."

She nodded, though she didn't know what she should be looking for.

They were escorted to a staircase that led to a windowed office. The small room was messy and the furniture old. Behind a large scarred oak desk a man in his late fifties with a full head of white hair regarded them with little warmth in his light-blue eyes. His brown suit was well tailored, its obvious cost at odds with the shabby conditions of the office. He steepled his well-manicured hands. "What can I do for you?" he asked, his accent heavy and foreign.

Brody's tense posture had Kate's nerves jumping.

"Are you Mr. Lanski?" Brody asked.

"I am. What do you want?"

"We're looking for information on a man named Paul Wheeler." Brody asked.

The man shrugged, his mouth pulling down at the corners. "I know no one by this name."

"How about Pete Kinsey?"

The older man's brow dipped together. "Again, I know no such person."

"Does the name Petrov ring any bells?"

The man waved a hand. "Petrov is a common name. I know nothing of these men. Now, I am a busy man. You go."

"Thank you for your time," Brody said as he ushered Kate out of the office and back through the warehouse to the street.

Kate breathed a sigh of relief to see the cab still sitting at the curb. As they slid into the backseat, she said, "That was a waste of time."

"Not so much. I think Mr. Lanski recognized all three names. Whether he knows the three are the same man remains to be seen."

She stared at him in surprise. "How can you tell?"

"It was in his eyes."

She processed that as the cab re-entered the steady flow of traffic. Brody asked the driver to take them to their original destination.

The taxi stopped in front of a five-story walk-up brownstone building. Kate climbed out of the cab and gazed around as Brody paid the fare.

Off in the distance, the concrete skyline of New York City rose sharply to the clouds. Kate took in the sights and sounds of the colorful neighborhood. Old men with round, craggy faces peered at them as they shuffled by. Several men wore medals attached to the lapels of their shirts.

Her heart stuttered at a long-forgotten memory. She had found a star-shaped medallion by accident once in Paul's belongings when they were moving into their shared apartment. He said the medallions had been given to those who'd fought for Russia long ago.

At the time she hadn't thought twice about how he knew this. She'd asked how he'd acquired the piece and had accepted his answer, that a client had given it to him. But his knowledge and his possession of the medallion made sense now that she knew he had some connection to that country.

Possibly a close connection.

That medallion now rested in a shoebox along with Paul's watch, wedding band and gold money clip. Anger moved through her, weakening her desire to go any further.

Two young women pushed past her. They spoke in Russian, as did most of the residents of Brighton Beach.

Bold letters splashed across signs over stores and the sides of buildings: Cyrillic writing that she didn't understand.

She clutched her purse tighter to her side as if the small black leather bag could protect her in some way from the inevitable—facing the other woman in Paul's life. Had he given her the love and tenderness, the security, Kate had craved?

"Ready?" Brody asked.

Somewhere inside the building before her was a woman who might possess the answers they sought. She wondered if her quest for the truth was about to end.

Would she finally be at peace or left more adrift? She gave Brody a tight smile. "I don't know if *ready* is the right word, but let's do this."

"You can handle it, Kate. You're strong."

His words warmed her heart. With him by her side she *could* do this. God had known she'd need someone to lean on. She said a silent prayer of praise and asked for God's strength.

Together they moved up the stairs. Brody pushed the button next to the name of the woman who'd written the letters. A garbled noise came from the intercom. Brody spoke into the square box. "We're looking for Olga."

A moment later, the front door buzzed. Brody opened the door and they stepped into the building's small foyer. Peeling blue paint and water-stained linoleum attested to the age of the place.

A television droned somewhere and the smell of cabbage sent Kate's nose twitching. Above them, a door opened with a squeak and then a blond woman leaned over the dark wooden stairwell railing. She was too far away for Kate to make out her features.

"Olga?" Brody asked.

"Yes." She stared at them warily, "What do you want?"

"We were hoping you could help us with something. May we come up?"

The woman didn't answer.

Kate tried to give a reassuring smile, though her insides were knotted up. She didn't want to do this, didn't want to face the woman Paul had had an affair with. But Kate would face her and the situation. She'd come this far; she had to see things through.

"We'll only take a few moments of your time," Kate offered.

Still, the woman only stared, as if trying to decide. "It's about Pau...Petrov," Kate said, past the lump in her throat.

The woman's eyes widened and she waved them up.

Kate glanced at Brody as they climbed the stairs. "Do you think she knows he's dead?"

"I hope so," he muttered.

"Me, too." She also hoped the woman already knew about her because Kate didn't want to be the one to deliver two devastating blows at once. His death would be enough of a shock.

On the fifth floor, they walked toward the open doorway of the last apartment. Music drifted out, teasing Kate's memory. She knew the tune. One of Paul's favorites. She swallowed past the hurt tightening her chest and sought Brody's gaze.

He placed his hand firmly on the small of her back, infusing her with the power necessary to walk into Paul's third life.

The apartment was a surprise. The muted burgundies and blues splashed throughout the living room created a homey and inviting atmosphere. White lace curtains hung over the single-paned windows, the mixture of Mission-style, sixties retro furniture and a smattering of antiques giving a hip, garage-sale impression, so unlike the rest of the building.

But it was the woman standing by the scarred, round oak table in the dining room who drew Kate's attention. Willowy and fragile, the tall blond blinked at them with trepidation. Her statuesque build and coloring were so different from Kate's. She didn't know if she'd have felt better about the other woman if they'd resembled each other.

"Olga, my name is Kate Wheeler and this is…my friend, Brody McClain."

"You know my Petrov? Is he safe? I have not heard from him in a long time." Her heavy accent rolled off her tongue in a lyrical cadence.

A sick feeling settled in the pit of Kate's stomach.

Shuffling footsteps came down the hall of the apartment. A tiny elderly woman, wearing a worn, faded orange housecoat and powder-blue slippers, stopped at the doorway to the living room.

The woman had Olga's blue eyes, but her stooped shoulders and wizened face led Kate to guess this must be Olga's grandmother. The woman eyed them curiously, then spoke to Olga in Russian. Whatever Olga said in return earned them a scowl.

"My grandmama does not approve of Petrov," Olga explained and then said something more to her grandmother, to which the elderly woman made a face and shuffled back down the hall.

Kate wished her own grandmother had been around to warn her away from Paul. Though she couldn't honestly say she'd have listened, as Olga clearly hadn't. Paul had been so charming. Had appeared to be the kind of man who would give her the stable and secure life she'd dreamed of. If someone had warned her that he'd turn out to be such a louse, she'd have laughed. She wasn't laughing now.

Brody stepped forward. "Maybe you should sit down."

Olga frowned, her blue eyes wide with worry. "Tell me, please."

Brody glanced at Kate and she saw the same dread in his eyes that crept up her own spine.

"Olga," Kate said. "Petrov sent you a package. Do you still have it?"

Confusion entered Olga's eyes. "Yes. Where is Petrov?"

Kate hesitated, then said, "We have some bad news. The man you know as Petrov is…"

"Is dead," Brody finished for her, his tone expressionless. But his eyes held an anger toward Paul that touched Kate. Brody was angry on her behalf and on behalf of this young woman. She couldn't deny how good his support felt.

Olga blinked as huge tears welled in her eyes. "No. No, I don't believe you."

Kate forced the feelings Brody stirred within her to a far corner of her heart and took Olga by the hand, leading her to the dark blue couch. "I'm sorry we have to be the ones to tell you."

"Who are you? Why do you tell me this? Petrov cannot be dead. I'd know. My brothers would have told me. His mother would know."

Kate blinked, stunned by this revelation. "His mother?" She turned to Brody, who'd sat in a chair across from them. "Paul told me his parents were dead."

"Who is this Paul?" Olga's lower lip trembled. "What have you done with my Petrov?"

Pushing aside her own hurt and anger over her dead

husband's deceit, Kate took a deep breath. "Your Petrov was also Paul Wheeler, my husband." She didn't even try to explain about Pete Kinsey.

Olga dropped her chin and drew back. Her gaze darted between Kate and Brody. "You lie. This cannot be."

Kate dug in her purse for her wallet and pulled out her wedding picture. With shaky hands, she handed the photo to Olga.

Olga stared at the photo without taking it. Tears slipped down her face. "I do not understand."

"Nor do I." Kate sympathized with Olga, understood the pain of realizing she'd been deceived.

"Olga, we need the package that Petrov sent to you." Brody's words brought the situation back in focus for Kate.

"Please, Olga. It's very important. It may be the key to why Paul…Petrov was killed." She hated the way her voice wavered when she said his name.

"Why should I trust you? I should call my brothers." She rose.

Brody made a gesture of entreaty. "There's no reason why you should trust us. We're strangers to you. All we can say is that whoever killed Petrov is now after Kate. Will you please help us so we can stop them?"

Olga's gaze searched Kate's face. No doubt she was wondering about the bruises and the cut. It occurred to Kate that she and Brody could be putting Olga in danger now, as well. But the bad guys hadn't found the letter so they didn't know about Olga. At least so she hoped.

Olga gave a slight nod and then left the room, disappearing down the hall. They heard Olga speaking with her grandmother, their voices low, yet from the intensity, Kate guessed Olga was informing her grandmother of Petrov's death.

"You okay?" Brody asked.

Kate felt as though she'd hit a brick wall. Numb, dumbfounded, shocked. "I don't think I'll ever be okay again."

Brody took her hand. She sent up a silent prayer of thanks again for this man. She didn't know if she could have done this without him.

Olga returned carrying a small wrapped box. One that could easily hold a computer disk. "I was waiting for Petrov to return before I opened this. Those were his orders." She handed the box to Brody, who quickly dispensed with the paper. He opened the box and pulled out the contents.

A feminine gasp filled the air and Kate wasn't sure if it were her own or Olga's. As Olga reached for the stunning piece of jewelry that Brody lifted from the box, Kate turned away.

Just when she thought she couldn't hurt anymore, Paul still managed to reach out from the grave and slice a fresh wound to her soul. The jade-studded gold pendant was identical to one Paul had given to her on their wedding night.

"It's not here." Brody's frustration was evident in his tone.

Kate shut off her emotions and refocused on why they were there. "Olga, we're looking for a computer disk. Did Petrov have a computer here?"

"No. He did not work with computers."

"What did Petrov do?" Brody questioned.

Olga's slim shoulders rose and fell in a stiff shrug. "He worked with my brothers. He traveled."

Brody's dark eyes took on an intense light. "What's the name of the business and what is Petrov's family's name?"

"The company is Lanski Imports and Petrov Klein is...was his name."

Kate brows rose in surprise. She glanced at Brody. He gave her a meaningful look and a slow nod. Brody'd been right that Mr. Lanski at least knew the name Petrov and most likely had known of his aliases.

Olga sniffed back more tears. "We were to be married next year. My brothers promised Petrov could stop traveling."

As soon as the divorce was final and he could leave Los Angeles, Kate thought sourly and swallowed hard against the fresh taste of hurt.

"Do you have an address for his mother?" Brody asked.

She willed herself not to care as Olga gave Brody the information he wanted. Paul/Pete/Petrov was a rat and she would not waste any more pain on him or his memory. She hated hurting like this, hated that she'd so easily allowed herself to be sucked into this horrible mess.

Never again. Never again would she allow anyone close enough to hurt her so much.

Brody recaptured her hand and Kate turned to stare into his eyes. She wondered bitterly which was worse: being used by her dead husband or the pity so clear in Brody's gaze.

* * *

Brody watched the shuttered look come over Kate and an ache deep inside twisted and squirmed. They'd received as much information as they were going to get from Olga. He rose and pulled Kate to her feet then quickly led her out, leaving behind a tearful Olga in the arms of her elderly grandma.

Once outside, Kate stepped away from him, her arms wrapping around her middle as she stared up the street. Brody sensed she wasn't seeing the hustle and bustle of pedestrians or taking in the ambiance of Little Odessa.

He touched her arm. She looked at his hand before lifting her gaze. He sucked in a quick breath at the desolate expression in her eyes. She couldn't be acting.

"I was such an imbecile," she said, her voice full of self-loathing.

"No. *He* was the imbecile." If the man weren't already dead, Brody would've taken great joy in torturing him.

"I don't understand. Why did he marry me? What plans did he have for me? For the woman up there?"

"I don't know. We may never know."

"That's unacceptable." Her hands clenched at her sides and her expression turned hard, unyielding. "I have to know."

Brody understood her frustration, her anger. The only advice he could give her was the same advice he'd heard and eventually had to learn to live with. "You have to let go of the questions and make peace with the unknown."

She scoffed softly. "How do I do that? How do I live with the knowledge that I trusted him, gave everything I had to my marriage, and there was never any hope? It was a sham from the beginning. How do I live with that?"

He grazed a knuckle down her soft cheek, wiping away a lone tear, the wetness hot against his skin. "You learn to live with it. Learn to focus instead on the needs of each day. You can't change the past and you can't control the future."

Her hot glare seared him. "That's easy to say. You've never had to go through something like this."

He let his hand drop to his side. "I have, Kate. I know what you're going through." Only too well.

"You do?"

He wasn't ready to open that particular door. "Come on, we should go."

She spun away from him. "You'll have to see his mother alone. I can't do that."

"I wouldn't ask you to."

He hated seeing the hard edges going up around her, hated knowing that she was cloistering her heart behind a stone wall composed of anger, hurt and mistrust. He knew how lonely that place was. He hated that the fire and sparkle that had first drawn him to her were dwindling.

He stepped closer and gently grasped her shoulders. She felt stiff, yet fragile, beneath his touch. "Don't do this, Kate. Don't let him hurt you anymore."

"I'd have to be able to feel to hurt."

Her icy tone sent a shiver moving along his spine like a storm blowing in from the Atlantic Ocean. He wasn't going to let her do this to herself. He wanted to see the spirited woman who'd fought him so bravely not that long ago. He turned her to face him. "Come on. I know you still feel something. Tell me you don't feel the sparks between us."

His words startled the coldness in her eyes back a step. Good. He wanted to chase that freezing bitterness as far away as he could. He refused to look too closely at why he felt the need to do so. "Tell me you don't wonder what it would be like to kiss me."

She blinked. Twin stains of pink spread across her cheeks. "Kiss you?"

"I've wondered, Kate. Would your lips be as soft as they look? Would you taste as sweet as the lilacs I smell in your hair?"

She tried to move away, but he held her firmly. Her gaze lifted. Beneath the hurt, an underlying current shimmered in the depths of her eyes. Her vulnerability stabbed at him, making his chest ache.

He silenced the voice inside his brain that warned he was getting in too deep. That warned he shouldn't trust.

His lips descended and met Kate's. Ripples of shock washed over him. She wasn't soft and pliant, she was hard as steel and just as strong, and she held herself at a distance from the flame ignited between them as if she were afraid of being burned.

He understood because he felt the same way. Drawn, yet terrified of the conflagration searing the air around them, between them. But he couldn't have pulled away even if the fire department had arrived to spray them with cold water.

He slid a hand from her shoulder to tangle in the mass of curls at the back of her head. Gently he caressed and massaged the tense muscles at the nape of her neck while he gentled his kiss.

She met his kiss with one of her own. His mind nearly exploded when that melting turned into a caress, her lips now receptive and sweet. He'd have sworn he could hear fireworks filling the sky.

Cement chips hit his legs with a sharp sting. Not fireworks. Gunfire.

ELEVEN

Deeply ingrained instincts kicked in and a familiar flood of adrenaline rushed through his blood. He pulled Kate down to the ground, covering her body with his own as his hand reached for the weapon holstered at his back.

A woman screamed, pedestrians ran for cover. Another round hit the pavement inches from his head and he flinched away from the flying shards of concrete. Time to move.

He pushed upward. "Come on!" In a low crouch, Brody hustled Kate to the shelter of a car. "Stay down!" he ordered.

Ignoring the swelling pain in his hip from the uncomfortable position, he peered over the back end of the tan sedan. His gaze roamed over the opposite sidewalk, along the storefronts and to the roof. There. Sunlight glinted off metal. Another round buried itself in the trunk of the car.

They had to get out of there. Brody looked for an escape. The B and Q subway station was a half block away. If they could make it across the street, the sniper wouldn't have as clear a shot.

The rumble of an approaching train reached him. Brody squatted beside Kate with his back leaned against the car's door, putting his weight mostly on his bent left leg. Kate was tucked in a ball. She peeked up at him through a veil of red curls.

"We've got to make a break for it, cross the street and go to the subway. Think you can do it?"

She blinked rapidly. Her chin lifted and she gave a shaky nod. Admiration arced through him. He knew she was scared, but she wasn't giving into her fear. *Atta girl.*

Taking her hand, Brody pushed away from the car, aiming his weapon at the man on the roof. "Go! Stay low!"

He squeezed off two rounds as he ran. Kate followed closely on his heels. More shots hit the ground, but they reached the other side of the street unharmed. Side by side, they ran toward the metal staircase leading up to the raised platform of the subway station. Their labored breaths mingled, drowning out the sounds of the approaching train.

People moved aside, giving barely curious glances as they ran past. With more finesse than he thought himself capable of, Brody jumped over the turnstile and then helped Kate scramble over.

"Hey!" shouted the token booth clerk from within her enclosed stall.

"Shots fired! Call 911!" Brody yelled.

With a loud swoosh and forceful current of air, the silver train roared into the station. Still clutching Kate's hand, Brody pushed their way to the last car and into the corner facing away from the station. He remained standing, while she sat on the bench.

Long moments passed as they waited for the metallic ding-ding that announced the imminent closure of the doors. Brody's watchful gaze searched for the unknown enemy through the window. Hopefully, the gunman on the roof had been alone. He didn't see anything that would lead him to believe they'd been followed. Who had known they were in Brighton Beach? Had they been tracked from Havensport?

The door closed and the train moved forward, picking up speed to rush over Brighton Beach toward Manhattan. Brody sank onto the seat beside Kate, his tension receding slightly even as his hip throbbed a sporadic beat. He glanced at Kate. Her chalky complexion and wide eyes as she stared out the window made Brody gather her into his arms. She shook violently and he expected hysterics. "Are you hurt?"

"No." She tilted her head back to look up at him, her gaze clear and sharp with intelligence. "And I thought things couldn't get any worse. Thank You, God, for my protector."

"Some protector," he muttered. If he'd been paying attention instead of kissing Kate, she wouldn't have come so close to being shot.

Kate twisted around to face him fully. "I'd have been toast a long time ago if it weren't for you."

Grateful to see her pluck returning, Brody gave her a grim smile and tightened his hold. "You're one incredible lady."

And if he wanted her to stay that way he had to start

doing his job and control his attraction to Kate. Otherwise, he might just get them both killed.

Kate followed Brody from subway to subway until they reached Penn Station. She looked around with interest. She'd never been to the fabled train depot before and was surprised to see it had the same grime and grit as any station, only with a greater number of people filing in and out due to the commuter and Amtrak trains.

On the walls were pictures of how Penn Station had looked before the deconstruction in the sixties. Kate felt a pang of regret for the architecture and beauty of the old station. Brody ushered her quickly to the ticket agent's booth.

He purchased two tickets for a private compartment on a train bound for Boston. She kept glancing over her shoulder expecting to see armed men bearing down on them.

She urged Brody to call N.Y.P.D. in case the subway attendant hadn't, and ask for someone to check on Olga. Kate couldn't live with herself if the danger following her harmed someone else. He led her to a pay phone where he made the call, because he had no cell phone service in the station.

They boarded the train and settled in the private compartment: a small cubicle with a window, two red-leather benches facing each other and an overhead storage area. Soon the rhythm of the steel wheels vibrated through the floor and lulled Kate's frazzled senses.

Somebody had shot at her.

The frightening reality was much worse than any melodrama she'd ever imagined.

She sank back onto the cushioned bench, which was more comfortable than she'd thought it would be when she'd entered the compartment. For one person, the space would have been roomy, but Brody's presence filled the small cubicle. Now an intimate atmosphere charged the close quarters.

He sat opposite her, his long legs stretched out between them, his big body leaned back and his strong arms, arms that had held her so close, so gently, folded across his broad chest. He studied her with hooded eyes. Her gaze dropped to his lips and heat crept into her cheeks.

She felt awkward after their kiss. *Explosive* didn't do justice to the kiss and the connection she felt. She *had* wondered what it would be like to kiss him, and it was more wonderful than she could have imagined. Brody's touch had awakened a yearning she'd never known before. A yearning that, if she gave in to it, could destroy what little remained of her self-respect.

Deep down, the craving to be loved and cherished sat with her like a stubborn child refusing to give up a favored toy. Brody had undoubtedly kissed her to distract her from her pain over Paul, not because he cared. She had to remember that.

She fidgeted under his regard and couldn't take the silence anymore. "Why Boston?"

"I have friends in Boston who will help us," Brody replied, his expression unreadable.

She remembered he wasn't from Havensport. "Are you from Boston?"

He nodded.

When he didn't offer anymore, Kate pressed, "There's someone there you trust?"

"My ex-partner."

Kate absorbed that tidbit. "So you were on the force in Boston?"

"Yeah."

"What took you to Havensport?"

One solid shoulder rose and fell. "They needed a sheriff."

Frustrated by his lack of cooperation in keeping the conversation going, she prodded, "So you decided to give up being a...detective?"

He nodded. "Homicide."

Kate drew back. Everything inside her flinched. Homicide. Murder. Her husband. Thoughts tumbled around her head. A flutter of panic hit her stomach. Surely he couldn't suspect her after all that had happened. She had to believe that her trust wasn't misplaced because if it were...she'd be certifiable. Just lock her up and throw away the key.

No, she was being paranoid. Brody wouldn't be helping her if he believed she was guilty of murdering her husband. With effort she continued the conversation. "So you gave up being a homicide detective to become sheriff of a small, sleepy, coastal town?"

His mouth quirked. "Something like that."

"Why?"

His only response was a raised brow.

Obviously, she wasn't getting anything more out of him. Ever since they'd made it safely to the subway, Brody had been quiet. He seemed more withdrawn than she'd seen him before.

One moment he was holding her in a safe and secure cocoon and the next he was sitting stiffly beside her, his gaze barely touching her. And when it did, the reticence in his dark eyes made fresh tears sting the back of her throat.

She didn't blame him for resenting her. He wouldn't have almost been killed and wouldn't be running now if she'd just agreed to let him call the FBI. Though she knew if Brody had really wanted the FBI's help, he would have called them regardless of her wishes.

He wasn't a man who let others make decisions for him. He was a man of action. A lawman. Living a risky, unsecured life. Even as a small-town sheriff, he faced the unknown every day.

Her mind replayed the events of the last few hours. The woman her husband had been involved with wasn't some tramp. She'd been in love, planning for a future. Paul had used Olga, too. Kate felt sorry for her. The young woman didn't deserve to be lied to. But then, neither had she. Bitter anger rooted around, trying to find a spot to plant itself.

As she stared at the man across from her, his intense eyes unreadable, his jaw set in a firm line, she remembered his words.

You have to let go of the questions and make peace with the unknown...learn to live with it. I have... I know what you're going through.

He'd indicated once he didn't trust in God to care, so how could Brody really have any peace? What kept him from leaning on God? Only one way to find out. "What happened to you, Brody? You said you know what I'm going through. How? What unanswered questions have you tried to make peace with?"

He didn't move. The only indication that he'd heard her was his slight, indrawn breath. Kate studied him, learning his face, seeing the subtle changes as he thought about how to answer. He blinked, a slow sweep of black lashes over high cheekbones. Kate's gaze rested on his mouth, the strong, hard lips that could be so tender.

She wanted Brody to let her in, to open up to her, to prove that he trusted her and believed in her. She wanted to be friends.

Friends were all they could ever be.

She'd just have to make sure her heart understood that she was never going to fall in love with Sheriff Brody McClain. The life of a cop's or sheriff's wife was the antithesis of what she wanted—security, peace.

Too bad the rest of her longed for the comfort and care she'd found in his arms.

Suddenly Brody had the distinct feeling that the private compartment had been a mistake. They were too close, too alone and all of his senses were on alert. He was attuned to every move, every breath she took. It would be too easy to forget his job and take up where they'd left off before the bullets had started flying. He'd never protect her that way. The latest near miss was proof enough.

Now Kate was asking him pointed questions about his past that he had no intention of answering. He couldn't let his guard down; he couldn't succumb to the connection arcing between them because the only way never to risk getting hurt again was not to love again.

He remained motionless under her emerald gaze.

Her eyes narrowed. "Does it have anything to do with your limp?"

He forced himself to remain expressionless even though her question seared him clean through. Of course, she'd have noticed his limp, which had become more pronounced over the course of the day. But had she noticed it before then? He stretched nonchalantly and shifted on the seat, taking some of the pressure off his sore hip. Why was he trying so hard not to reveal his injury to Kate?

Pride.

He didn't want her to view him as weak. How could she trust him to protect her if she knew he could no longer pass muster as a detective?

Kate moved from her seat and sat beside him on the padded bench seat. "You told me not to let Paul win by allowing him to hurt me anymore. Don't you think it's time you stopped letting your past win?"

His own words were coming back to haunt him. He gave her a hard glance. "You know nothing about my past."

"And you know everything about mine. Doesn't seem fair." She made an impatient gesture with her hands, her knuckles brushing against his leg.

Running a hand through his hair, Brody tried to

ignore the prickles of awareness coursing through him at Kate's unintentional touch. "Telling you won't change anything."

"No, probably not."

Surprised by her bluntness, he turned to face her. Her eyes were closed, her head leaned back against the wall, her lips slightly parted as if waiting for his kiss.

Abruptly, he stood, his head hitting the low ceiling. He winced. "I'm going to find some food."

Kate opened her eyes and regarded him steadily, her gaze telling him she knew exactly what he was doing. Running away from her uncomfortable questions, running away from her.

"Why are you doing this, Brody?"

He raised a brow. "I'm hungry?" he said, trying for levity.

Her lush mouth quirked. "I mean, why are you helping me? What's in it for you?"

Good question. A question that Brody had ignored from the get-go. Part of why he felt compelled—and that was a good description—to help Kate stemmed from some twisted need for redeeming his judgment. Somehow, by helping Kate, he could prove he wasn't a sucker for a pretty face and that he was now capable of determining the innocent from the guilty.

Then there was Kate herself. Her kind and gentle spirit, the spark of fire in her eyes, the way she looked at him with so much trust. Maybe it was because it felt so good to have her call him her guardian angel. If there were such a thing, Kate deserved one.

But so had his father, and there hadn't been one

around. Brody steered his memories away from the night his father had died and from the thoughts of faith Kate stirred within him.

Her trust in him made him want to answer, even if his answer wasn't the complete truth. He sat down and braced his elbows on his knees. "I'm helping you because it's my job to."

She leaned forward. Red curls bounced on her shoulders, her expression was determined. "That's not why. Maybe at first, but it doesn't fly now. You could have handed me off to the FBI. Why didn't you?"

"And miss all this fun?" He blinked at her innocently.

Kate gave an exasperated shake of her head. "Is your family in Boston?"

"Yes." Brody's mouth quirked in amusement at her change in tactics. She was a tenacious lady. He had a feeling she wouldn't let up until she got the answers she wanted both from him and from her dead husband. He admired her determination even as he deplored the foolhardiness of treading on dangerous ground. She shouldn't be here, putting herself in the line of fire, searching for shadows.

"Talking to you is like talking to a brick wall," Kate muttered.

Brody chuckled. "You sound like my little sister."

Kate arched a brow, encouraging him without words to continue. He never talked about his family or his life. In his job, he was the one to ask the questions. He felt awkward. It occurred to him that there was safety in his role. He mentally shrugged. Telling her about his family could only deepen her confidence in him to protect her.

"My mom still lives in the house I grew up in. I have three siblings. My older brother, Patrick, teaches at Boston College, my little sister, Meghan, runs an art gallery in New York City and my baby brother, Ryan, is an investment broker."

"Your dad?"

Brody stiffened.

"Divorce?"

He relaxed slightly at the tenderness in her tone. He remembered what she'd told him of her parents. "No, my parents had a happy marriage." The need to confide in her caught him by surprise and he couldn't hold back. "My father was a cop."

Kate swallowed hard. A sinking feeling pulled at her. "Was?"

Pain deepened the darkness of his eyes. "He was killed."

Compassion tightened a knot in Kate's stomach. "I'm sorry."

"Yeah, me, too."

He splayed his fingers through his hair. A wayward lock fell across his forehead. She resisted the urge to push it back in place. "Was he on duty?"

The corners of his mouth tightened. "No. He'd just come off his shift." Brody's eyes took on a faraway glaze. "I'd missed the bus, so Mom called Dad and had him come pick me up at school. We were on our way home."

The realization of where this story was going filled her with dread.

A sad smiled touched his lips. "He teased me about liking school so much that I'd want to spend the night. We both laughed because my older brother Patrick was the one passionate about school."

The smile faded. "A call came over the radio. Another cop was in trouble, needed backup. We were just around the corner. I remember he hit the steering wheel with the palm of his hand and I nearly jumped out the window. He had this expression on his face that I'd dubbed his cop look...angry, intense. He jerked the wheel. We shot down a side street. We were the first to arrive. The other cruiser was empty, the door wide open. He told me to stay put and lock the door. Then he got out."

The dread squeezed her insides. "You didn't stay put."

"I was twelve. I wanted in on the action, wanted to see my dad take down the bad guy." He clenched and un-clenched his fists. "Only I saw the bad guy take down my dad. The scum shot him in the chest. He died...in-stantly."

Her heart ached for the little boy who'd seen such violence, for the man who lived with the memory. No wonder he thought God didn't care. She touched his arm. The muscles beneath the cotton of his blue chambray shirt tensed. The naked anguish in his eyes hit Kate square in the chest.

"I'm so sorry, Brody. No one should witness that, let alone a child." She blinked back tears. "Why did you become a policeman?"

"To honor my father. To give to the department that gave so generously to our family." His jaw tightened. "To make sure the bad guys in this world paid for their crimes."

She squeezed his arm. "I admire you for that."

His hand closed over hers with unbearable tenderness. The expression in his fathomless eyes shifted. The pain receded. The inner light now in his eyes stalled her breath. She licked her lips. His gaze tracked the motion. Her heart hiccupped.

"I don't know why I told you." The husky timbre of his voice slid down Kate's spine, cementing the specialness of the moment. His story made her want to weep. His confidence moved her.

"Sometimes...it's good to talk," she murmured.

One side of his mouth cocked upward. "I've talked to more head doctors over the years than I have toes."

"That's a lot of doctors." Had he moved? His lips seemed so close.

"You should see my toes."

The vibrant tone in his whisper zinged through Kate. She dragged in a ragged breath. "As long as your feet don't smell."

Brody's rich laughter wrapped around her, releasing the pent-up energy charging the air between them.

Kate scooted away, allowing a cooling space to bring sanity back to the situation. "Did you say something about food?"

His amused gaze let her know he realized she was using his avoidance tactic. Embarrassment flushed through her. He stood and held out his hand. She allowed him to pull her to her feet and told herself to let go of his hand, but she couldn't quite find the power to release her hold on him as they went in search of the dining car.

She questioned her sanity. It was one thing to want the sheriff to believe her, to believe *in* her. And it was an entirely different thing to allow herself to bond to him. She would not fall for him, a man whose very job created insecurity.

TWELVE

Brody watched Kate from the corner of his eye. She stared out the window of the taxi, her eyes wide, taking it all in as they traveled down Summer Street.

"What a beautiful city," she commented as they crossed the Fort Point Channel.

His mouth twisted into a smile. He thought she was beautiful. Her hair, her eyes, her smile. There was no question the whole outside package was a work of art. But the real beauty lay within. There was beauty in her determination to see this ordeal through. Beauty in the resilience that kept her on her feet and moving. Beauty in her compassion and generosity to a woman who by all rights she should resent.

And her faith shone like a brilliant star, bringing light to even his darkened soul.

They were entering the area of Boston referred to as Southie. His part of town. The traffic slowed, became a crawl as they passed by heavy construction equipment and men wearing hard hats and orange vests. The work area seemed endless.

At her questioning glance, he said, "The Big Dig. The city's way of solving the increasing traffic problems. They're taking the highways underground."

The taxi moved forward, picking up speed as the traffic cleared. Brody watched his old haunts roll by. There was McGlinty's Tavern, the after-shifts hangout for several local precincts. On the corner was the movie theater, now expanded into a multiplex.

He'd known these streets so well. Grown up here, walked the same beat as his father before making detective. But all that went up in smoke one stormy night. His career stalled. His heart betrayed. His thoughts zeroed on the woman sitting beside him.

She'd gotten under his skin. That was the only explanation he could find for telling her about his father. He never spoke about that. Not even to Elise.

An uneasy feeling settled in the pit of his stomach. He shouldn't have let his guard down, he shouldn't have opened up to her, risking his heart. Risking betrayal. He wouldn't make the same mistake again.

No, he had a plan.

With the help of his ex-partner, they'd solve the mystery of Kate's husband and then he could get on with his life as sheriff without her.

But the thought of going back to his little studio apartment with its white, unadorned walls and cold hardwood floors didn't hold much appeal. Not when he could easily envision a home with Kate. A place where she would add feminine touches to make it cozy and warm, where her concern and affection would be his.

He frowned, not liking the direction his thoughts

were taking him. Playing house was not an option. Emotions wouldn't dictate his moves. He had a job to do. The job must always come first. Kate was a job. Nothing more.

"Is something wrong?" Kate's anxious whisper shook him from his thoughts.

"No. Everything's great." Even to his own ears he didn't sound very convincing. He gave her what he hoped was a reassuring smile.

Moments later the taxi pulled up in front of the South Boston police precinct where Brody and his father before him had once served the public. Brody's chest grew tight. He hadn't been back since the day he'd become sheriff of Havensport. Suddenly he missed the serenity of his small town.

He helped Kate from the car. The pulsing beat of the city filled his senses and the afternoon sun made the cotton of his shirt stick to his skin. Kate's hand gripped his tightly. He saw the worry in her bright-green eyes. He squeezed her hand as he led her up the concrete steps toward the glass doors of the redbrick station house.

Once inside, Brody took a moment to absorb the familiarity of the precinct.

The soothing salmon tones of the marble-tiled walls reflected the light coming through the windows. His gaze took in the black-and-gold plaques spread out across the walls. His father's name was on the plaque near the top left-hand corner. He'd looked up to his dad when he was alive. It only seemed right that he could still look up to him.

Brody took a step forward. A twinge of pain shot up his leg, acutely reminding him he'd come close to having his own plaque etched with his name on that wall.

"McClain!" A gray-haired uniformed police officer charged forward with an outstretched hand. "As I live and breathe…I'd given up thinking we'd see you here again."

"Captain." Brody clasped Sean O'Grady's hand and was unceremoniously pulled into his father's old friend's embrace.

"Does your mother know you're in town, boy?"

"Not yet, but I'm sure she will soon."

From the twinkle in Sean's eyes, Brody had no doubt Colleen McClain would be receiving a phone call within minutes of her son's arrival. Though his father had been gone for years, the sense of family and community in the department continued for the widow and children when one of their own died in the line of duty.

Sean's gaze settled on Kate, who stood quietly to Brody's left. The curiosity and speculation glinting in the old man's eyes brought heat creeping up Brody's neck.

"This is Kate Wheeler," Brody said.

"Ma'am." Sean inclined his head and then turned questioning eyes to Brody.

"She's…uh…in my protective custody."

Bushy gray brows rose. "Your custody, eh? Didn't know sheriffs did that sort of thing."

Irritation burned its way into Brody's chest. Everyone on the force knew why he'd left; he didn't want them thinking history was repeating itself, that he was falling for another suspect. "Is Gabe around?"

Sean gestured with his hand toward the back of the station. "At his desk."

"Thanks." Brody grasped Kate by the elbow and pulled her with him away from Sean's scrutiny.

As they moved through the station, a sense of welcome wrapped around him as he acknowledged shouts of greeting and waves from fellow officers he'd once served with. He forced his mind not to dwell on why he'd left or on how good it felt to be back.

At the rear of the station house, past several rows of desks, sat his ex-partner, Gabriel Burke.

At one time Brody had been closer to Gabe than he'd been to his own two brothers, until Brody's stubborn defense of Elise had wedged a wall between them. A wall that remained today, five years later.

Brody braced himself as they approached Gabe and he met his ex-partner's wary hazel gaze. Gabe had aged. There were lines on his chiseled face that hadn't been there before and a few distinctive gray hairs at his temple.

Pleasure crowded Brody's chest. He quickly forced his emotions under control as he said, "Hey, Gabe."

"McClain." Gabe's gaze slid over Kate, over the hand with which Brody still held her elbow and back to meet Brody's eyes.

Brody stiffened at Gabe's silent reprimand, but he didn't release Kate. He'd stand behind his decision to help her without apology. "We need your help."

"Picking out china?"

"With a police matter," Brody stated firmly.

Gabe sat back and crossed his massive arms over his barrel chest. "Just can't keep yourself from getting mixed up with women who can ruin your career, now, can you, Brody?"

The air swooshed out of Brody's lungs as if he'd taken a shoulder in the gut. Apparently, securing his friend's help wasn't going to be as easy he'd anticipated.

Kate felt Brody flinch. She glanced up to see his strong jaw tighten and his eyes narrow with suppressed hostility. Nervousness roiled in her stomach. What was going on? Why were they so angry at each other? Who was this other woman Gabe mentioned? Brody's career ruined?

"Don't start with me, Gabe," Brody warned.

Gabe raised his hands, callused palms facing out. "Hey, I'm just stating the obvious."

"This is different."

Curious, Kate held her breath as the two men stared at each other for a long charged moment, then Gabe's gaze shifted to her. He was a good-looking man around Brody's age—midthirties, she'd guess—with a square jaw and light blond hair, though there was a hardness to Gabe that made her shiver. She lifted her chin beneath his uncomfortable scrutiny.

Gabe shrugged his massive shoulders as he once again turned his attention back to Brody. "Not according to the FBI."

Brody jerked his hand away, leaving Kate slightly off balance. A flutter of panic sent ripples up her spine.

"The Feds contacted you? Why?"

The thread of suspicion in Brody's voice made Kate pull her bottom lip between her teeth.

Gabe's gaze narrowed. "They know she's with you.

They figured you'd contact me." One corner of his mouth curled upward. "And here you are. Seems they think *she*—" he nodded his blond head in Kate's direction "—possesses the information that could blow apart an international money-laundering scam."

A hot wave of shame and anger hit Kate. Not only had Paul been a liar but also a thief. And she'd never known.

Brody's gaze locked with hers. She couldn't read his thoughts; he'd put on that impassive cop face that she didn't like. She shook her head. "I don't have any information."

"The disk," Brody said sharply, his expression intent.

Her defenses kicked in. "I don't have it," she replied just as sharply.

His expression softened and he took her hand. "I know."

The comfort from his touch and the relief his unexpected words produced made her thankful she was firmly anchored to him or she'd have floated to the ceiling. She gave him a grateful smile.

Gabe sat forward. "What's this about a disk?"

Brody explained what had happened in the last few days. As she listened, Kate marveled at how good it felt to know Brody trusted her, believed her. She was truly blessed to have had God bring him into her life, even if there was no future for them together. As a couple.

She couldn't contemplate living the life of an officer's wife. She just couldn't. It was too risky and uncertain. Law officers faced death on a regular basis. And one day, death could win.

Gabe blew out a harsh breath. "What do you want me to tell the Feds? They want her brought into custody."

Gabe's question brought Kate's attention back to the situation. Her throat constricted, trapping her breath. For a moment the room spun. She held on tightly to Brody.

"Nothing yet." His thumb rubbed her palm in a reassuring manner. The panic quieted, but a whole other maelstrom of sensation started sliding through her blood as air filled her lungs. She really liked how easily he was able to calm her fears. She took a quick breath.

"I need your help to look into this import business her husband was involved with," Brody said.

Gabe studied her, but addressed Brody. "Are you sure you want to do this, Brody? You could hand her over to the Feds and be done with it. They'd protect her, they'd find the answers." He released Kate's gaze to turn to Brody. "You sure you want to go down this road again? Remember where it led last time."

A quick parade of anger and bitterness crossed Brody's features before he subdued his reactions into his normal impassive demeanor. "Like I said. This is different."

"Yeah." The corners of Gabe's mouth lifted into a humorless attempt at a smile. "Let's hope so."

Brody's jaw visibly tightened.

Gabe turned to the computer, his fingers tapping at the keys. "What are we looking for?"

Brody turned to Kate and indicated an empty desk adjacent to Gabe's. "Have a seat."

Feeling out of place and unneeded, she sat and

watched the two men. One dark, one light. Both were big and strong-looking and exuded an air of confidence that she guessed came with the badge. She didn't much like the way Gabe assessed her as if she were gum stuck to his shoe, something he wished his friend would avoid.

She knew Brody wouldn't tell her what their coded conversation was about. She gathered a woman had hurt Brody once. The thought twisted inside her chest. He was a good man, and the more she knew of him, the more complex and interesting he became. And the more threatening to her heart.

Kate rested her elbow on the desk and placed her chin in her hand. The adrenaline from the day seeped out of her. She blinked several times, trying to fight the exhaustion, but she was losing the battle, just as she was with her growing feelings for Brody.

"Hey, your girlfriend's falling asleep at my desk."

Brody yanked his gaze away from the information on the computer screen and swung around to look at the dark-haired female officer he didn't recognize. She stared back at him with a raised brow. He shifted his gaze to Kate, who was slumped over the desk, her red curls spilling in disarray around her shoulders, her face relaxed and unguarded.

"She's not my girlfriend," he said even as something warm and tender expanded in his chest. He frowned at the unfamiliar sensation and checked his watch. He and Gabe had been at it for a long time, and what they'd found had him narrowing his gaze back on Kate. How could she not have known?

"Well, you going to move her or what?" the woman said.

"Cut'em some slack, there, Angie," Gabe said.

Brody stood, taking his weight on his good leg. "We'll be out of your way in a sec."

He went to Kate and gently shook her shoulder. Her hair slid over his hand like a caress. His insides clenched and if they weren't in a public place he would have been seriously tempted to slide her hair farther away from her neck and kiss the spot where her pulse visibly beat beneath her pale skin. Instead, he said, "Kate, wake up."

She stirred and raised her head. Her unfocused gaze looked frantically around before she blinked up at him. "What happened?"

He reflexively touched her cheek. "You fell asleep."

She straightened and looked over his shoulder to the female officer standing behind him. "Sorry."

Angie shrugged. "No big deal."

Brody helped Kate to her feet. She adjusted the strap of her purse and gazed up at him expectantly. Since they hadn't planned on an extended trip to New York or the need to travel to Boston, they hadn't packed any clothes. He made a decision. "I'm taking you to my mother's."

A scoffing noise behind them set Brody's nerves on edge. He turned to glare at Gabe, who arched an innocent brow.

"We're not returning to Havensport?" Kate asked.

"Not yet." He turned again to Gabe. "Contact me if you find out any more info."

Gabe's intense gaze bore into him. "And the Feds?"

Brody couldn't ask his friend to lie for him. "Do what you will."

Gabe rolled his eyes. "I hope you know what you're doing."

Brody inclined his head but refrained from letting loose with the words *me, too.* He knew he was doing the right thing by trusting Kate.

And if he wasn't? What then?

As Kate followed Brody back through the station and out to the sidewalk, she couldn't help noticing there was something on his mind. She'd caught a glimpse of uncertainty in his dark gaze at Gabe's parting comment. She didn't appreciate Gabe resurrecting doubts in Brody's mind that she'd been working so hard to banish.

With his hand to the small of her back, Brody steered her around a few pedestrians and guided her toward the park across the street. The warm, late-summer air pressed in on her. Beads of perspiration formed on the back of her neck beneath her hair and soaked into her shirt. "Could we stop at a store so I can buy some clothes?"

One corner of Brody's mouth raised in a small smile. "I'm sure Meggie has something you can borrow."

"Meggie?"

"My little sister."

"Oh, right." Nervous butterflies kicked up their wings in her stomach. She was going to meet his family. What did that mean?

She tried not to let her imagination run amok with thoughts that he cared for her and wanted his family's approval. More likely he didn't know what else to do with her, where else to take her and keep her safe. Because she didn't doubt for a minute that Brody would continue to protect her. He'd given his word. Brody was a man full of honor and integrity.

But the thought of meeting his family still sent anxiety weaving around her heart. She had enough vanity to want to make a better impression on Brody's family than she had on Gabe.

"Where is your mother's house?" she asked, wondering why they were walking through the park.

Off to one side, a playground teeming with children filled the air with merry noise. A woman walking a poodle passed by and the little white fluff sniffed at Kate's feet before moving on.

"Our house is on the west end of the park."

They neared a small stream that flowed beneath a stone footbridge. As they crested the slight rise in the middle of the walkway, Brody captured Kate's hand and pulled her to the side. Her breath tripped and her senses perked up.

Releasing her hand, Brody said, "I have to tell you what I found out about your husband."

She leaned her hips against the railing and stared out over the lush green meadow, cut down the center by the trickling stream. A gentle breeze sent the leaves of the trees swaying into motion.

Kate watched the way the sun peeked in and out through the tree branches. She didn't want Brody to continue. Her quest for the truth was wearing her down. Why couldn't it all just go away? But it wouldn't. She knew peace would only come with the truth, so she braced herself for more. "Okay, what now?"

His gaze narrowed slightly. Watchfulness stole into his expression. "With the information Olga gave us, Gabe and I were able to find out more about Paul Wheeler. His true name was indeed Petrov Klein. He was born in Brighton Beach to Russian immigrants."

So Olga had known the real man.

Kate had been thoroughly conned. She shook her head in disgust and anger. She worked hard to keep the bitterness at bay.

"The Klein family and the Lanski family are both linked to what the media refers to as the Russian Mob."

Kate blinked. "Mob?"

"The *Organizatsiya*. Russian organized crime. Similar to the Italian Mafia, only worse in some ways. More educated and technically skilled. Petrov went to Yale, learned how to manage money and was put to working with the Lanskis' import business. The company is just this side of legit so the Feds can't shut it down.

"Petrov disappeared from the Feds' radar about six years ago and apparently reemerged three years ago as Pete Kinsey, aka Paul Wheeler. The Feds think Petrov was getting tired of the game and wanted out. Maybe he threatened to expose the operation he was involved in. So they killed him. Now the Russians want the disk he'd put the incriminating information on."

Her mind reeled. Russian Mafia? A tight fist of rage

lodged itself in her middle. She gazed up at Brody, beseeching him to make all this comprehensible. "I don't understand. How do I fit into this?"

"The bank you work for is connected through various channels to a Russian bank."

Kate put her cold hands to her face and looked away. "The bank?" It made a twisted kind of sense. "No wonder he'd been so gung-ho about my career. But how could my working for the bank help him? Them?"

At Brody's silence, she raised her gaze back to his. His guarded expression forced the breath from her lungs. She dropped her hands and faced him fully. "You can't possibly think I have anything to do with the Russian Mob."

His gaze searched her face. "Did you suspect anything at all? Did he ever slip into Russian when angry?"

"No!" She felt like she was treading water in a whirlpool. "I thought you believed in me."

"I want to, Kate."

She balled her fists at her sides as helpless fury volleyed with indignation. "Then do. It's a matter of choice, Brody. Don't doubt me now, please." She had to have his reassurance. Though her faith would sustain her, she needed Brody's trust to hang on to as an anchor in the storm her life had become.

She prayed Brody wouldn't let her drown.

THIRTEEN

"It's not you I doubt, Kate. It's my own judgment."

Kate's fists relaxed slightly as an anxious ripple began somewhere in the vicinity of her heart. "Because some woman once betrayed you."

He flinched. "How did you…?"

"It wasn't too hard to read between the lines. Gabe's worried you're making the same mistake. What mistake?"

He frowned. "It doesn't matter."

"Yes, it does. This is my life that hangs in the balance. We've come this far, don't shut me out." Her heart ached in her chest. Her heart also hung in the balance.

He let out a heavy breath, his expression shifted, revealing his torment. "I became…involved with a suspect."

"Involved how?" she asked softly.

He met her gaze straight-on, his eyes full of bitter recrimination. "I fell hard."

Deep inside she responded to his pain. She also felt

the sting of self-reproach for falling in love with Paul. "She didn't share your feelings?"

He laughed, a caustic noise that burst from his chest. "I thought she did, up until the moment she shot me."

She gasped, the air trapped painfully in her chest. He'd faced death at the hands of someone he'd loved. "Oh, no."

Her shocked response seemed to make him angry.

His lips, lips that could be so gentle, twisted into a harsh grimace. "Don't feel sorry for me, Kate. It's my own fault. I was too blind to see what everyone else saw so plainly. Too stubborn to listen."

She put a hand on his arm. The muscles flexed beneath her touch. "We're quite a pair. Here, I thought I'd cornered the market on bad judgment. Never looking beyond the surface. Seeing only what I wanted to see. Paul used me and I didn't even know it."

He ran a gentle finger down her cheek. The caress made her long for more of his touch. "You took your husband at face value, trusted him, as you should have. He's at fault, not you." His hand fell away. "I, on the other hand, should have known. It was a mistake that nearly cost me my life. It cost me my career."

She frowned. "They asked you to leave?"

He stared off into the distance, his expression drawn, showing the hurt that still lingered. "No, not in so many words. I was taken off the street. Relegated to a desk job."

She knew how devastating that must have been for a man who'd gone into law enforcement to honor his father. It hit her that he'd lost his father and his career for not heeding the warnings given. Had those warnings come from God? Was that the wall that stood between Brody and God's grace?

She ached for Brody in a way she'd never ached for anyone else. She wanted to heal him, to help find his way back to God. She want to love him.

Shying away from that last dangerous thought, she reached for him, wrapping her arms around his middle and laying her head against his chest.

He stiffened for a moment and she froze, thinking he'd push her away. But then his arms enfolded her in a warm embrace. She listened to the beat of his heart, took comfort from his embrace. Breathed in the mingling mix of scents clinging to him: the musky scent of man, the remnants of his aftershave and the smell of sunshine and earth from the park.

She leaned back to look up into his face. "You haven't lost everything, Brody. You're still sheriff, that's got to count for something."

His tender smile played across her senses like fingers strumming a guitar, making her body hum. "It does." A shadow passed over his face and the smile faded. "As long as I don't make the same mistake."

A shaft of hurt streaked through her. She drew back, slipping her arms from around him. Her hands came to rest palms-down, flat against his chest. "So, if this woman betrayed you, used you... If she was so bad...then all women must be, is that it? Is that how I should feel, what I should think? That because Paul was such a rat, that all men are?"

The moment the words were out she realized that she could easily fall into that trap. Had started down that exact road. But Brody wasn't like that. He was good; he was sent by God to protect her. And she trusted him with her life. He'd already proved his honor to her.

He breathed out an audible breath. "No. I mean…it's not that simple."

"But it *is* that simple—and that complex at the same time. People have choices. God gave humans free will so we could choose. Choose to do right or wrong, choose to love Him or not. Choose to hurt others or not. It wasn't God's plan for you to be betrayed. It wasn't God's plan for your father to die. I know in my soul that God wept with you, Brody."

His heart thudded against her palms. In his gaze she saw his skepticism, his hurt and anger. Sadness rose up and choked her with tears.

Lead by example, Katie. The words spoken by her grandmother so long ago rang true in her head.

If she wanted Brody to believe in God's faithfulness then she needed to show him her own faith. "It wasn't God's plan for Paul to deceive me. I know He's as angry as I am. But He promises to use all things for good for those who love Him. I love Him, Brody, and I know there will be some good out of all this muck. I choose to believe that."

He shook his head, his gaze shifting away. "I don't have that kind of faith."

"You can choose to." She wanted to help him find his way to God, to healing because he'd always be running from his guilt and shame otherwise.

He nudged her arms up so that she entwined them around his neck and then he pulled her closer as he leaned back against the stone railing of the footbridge. She nearly cried with the need to be loved, to be cherished. Her heart pounded so hard in her chest she figured any second a rib would snap.

He closed his eyes for a moment and when he opened them they were clear and focused on her. "You are an amazing lady, Kate Wheeler. You know just how to make a guy squirm."

A nervous laugh escaped her. "I'm not sure if that's a compliment or not."

He lowered his head. "It is."

His lips hovered above hers. His warm breath fanned out across her face. She dropped her gaze to his well-formed lips, and her own breath held somewhere between her heart and her throat.

She sensed he was waiting for her to make the next move, to meet him halfway. Did she dare? Did she want to deepen the connection between them when she knew she'd never allow it to go beyond a single kiss, beyond the point of needing his protection?

Because she wouldn't ask for his love.

He may not be an officer on the Boston police force but he was a lawman, a sheriff. She understood why he was an officer of the law, and she could never ask him to give that up. Nor could she live with it. She wanted normal, stable. No risks, no surprises. Peace and security.

But she also wanted Brody.

The dilemma left her head reeling. And with Brody crowding her senses, her rationale for not giving in to the moment paled to a paltry nuisance, like a mosquito flying about her head.

Lord, what do I do?

She searched her heart, hoping for some sign, some message telling her to back off or go ahead. There were only her feelings, her wants clamoring to be heard. But giving in to them would put her heart at risk. "Brody, we shouldn't…I can't. You're…"

"I'm what?"

His deep voice rasped across her senses, weakening her resolve. She took a shuddering breath. She wanted there to only be honesty between them. "There's no future for us, Brody. Your life is too full of danger. I can't be like my mother, always wondering, worrying if you'd come home at the end of the day. I want peace and security. You can't offer me that."

"No, I can't," he agreed, though his lips still hovered close, beckoning.

Yearning welled, urging her to take what he offered, if only for the moment. "We really shouldn't start something that we can't finish," she mused more to herself than to him.

He made a noise of agreement in his throat and then lifted his chin to softly press his lips to her forehead. The chaste kiss left her frustrated and yearning for what could never be.

"Like I said, an amazing woman." He released her and stepped away. "Let's go. I'm sure my mom is anxiously waiting for us."

She told herself she should be relieved and grateful he'd let her go so easily, but she couldn't help feeling as if she'd just let something wonderful slip through her grasp.

* * *

It wasn't God's plan.

Brody chewed on that statement as he eased Kate along the park's paved path toward his childhood home. Though his pulse had slowed to a normal rate, he had to force his mind to concentrate on the tidbit of wisdom Kate had doled out and not on the kiss they'd almost shared.

If it wasn't God's plan that his father die, that Brody would be betrayed by the woman he'd thought he'd loved, then why had they happened? Why did any of the bad things in life happen? Where was God's grace?

Kate talked about choices. Somewhere inside his soul he knew that to be true. Probably some long-forgotten Sunday-school lessons hidden deep in the recesses of his being. Church had been a constant in the McClain family for as long as he could remember. His mother still attended, but after his father's death, Brody couldn't go. He'd felt too hurt, too guilty to seek God.

But ever since Kate had stepped into his life, the faith he'd turned away from kept nudging at him, reminding him of the truths he'd learned as a boy. Reminding him of the betrayal he'd felt when his father died.

He still didn't understand God's plan. He wasn't sure he ever would or even if he wanted to. He didn't want his guilt confirmed. Didn't want to know that had he obeyed his father, his father would still be alive. He didn't deserve God's grace.

Kate stumbled on a rut in the blacktop path. Brody gripped her elbow tighter as she leaned into him for a moment. He caught a faint whiff of her lilac scent and thought of the freshness of spring. Her curves pressed into his side for a split second before she straightened and continued on. His mouth went dry.

He vividly remembered the feel of those curves, soft and yielding. She'd felt so good, so right in his arms. She made him feel alive.

She was right to call a halt to…he didn't even know what to call that moment on the bridge. Another lapse in judgment? How many times was he going to ignore his vow not to let her in, to let her close?

Kissing her again would have been a huge mistake. Because this time it would have been from wanting her rather than hoping to distract her. And wanting her was not something he intended to let happen. Not again.

He looked up and found they'd come to the edge of the park and stood on the sidewalk facing the two-story home he'd grown up in. His chest tightened. As a boy running home from the park he'd never taken the time to notice how colorful his mother's flowers were, nor how comforting it was to have a place to come home to, to feel safe in.

Comfort welled up and clogged his throat. All the good memories in his life were here in this house. It had taken time away for him to really appreciate the life his mother had worked so hard to provide for her children after his father's death.

"Brody?" Kate's uncertain, tentative expression tugged at his heart.

He smiled with reassurance. "The white house with the green shutters and the tall oak in the front yard. That's where I grew up." He pointed to the second-story window on the right. "My brothers and I shared that room."

"Is that one of your brothers there, by the black car?"

Noticing the black BMW sedan parked on the street, Brody raised a brow. His younger brother leaned against the side of the car, dressed in his uniform, a dark blue pin-striped suit and red tie. He held a cell phone to his ear in one hand while the other hand gestured wildly to punctuate whatever he was saying.

Brotherly love gripped Brody. He hadn't realized how much he'd missed his siblings. "Yes, that's Ryan, the financial mogul. He's also the baby in the family." His little brother who'd followed him around, dogging his steps. "Only don't let him know I said that. The last time I referred to Ryan as the baby, we both came away from the ensuing scuffle with black eyes and bruised egos."

Kate chuckled. "I won't tell."

They crossed the street. Brody's first inclination was to guide her straight up the front stairs and into the house to avoid the inevitable questions from his little brother about the pretty woman on his arm, but Ryan waved to him and Brody resigned himself to engaging with his gregarious younger sibling.

Brody didn't know why he'd thought he'd be able to bring Kate home without being grilled like a fish on the barbecue. His family was all about sharing the details. Something he'd not relished growing up.

Kate stepped off to the side by the gate as Brody moved closer to the black car.

"We'll close at half a mil and no less." Ryan made a face at the person on the phone. "Think about it. We'll talk tomorrow. Gotta go." He clicked his phone closed and shook his head before slipping the small silver technological wonder into the breast pocket of his suit jacket. Pleasure lit up his brown gaze. "Well. Are my eyes deceiving me or is that my big brother?"

"One of them," Brody responded drily.

Ryan came off the car in a flash, his facing breaking into an easy smile as he engulfed Brody in a bear hug. "Mom's going to be beside herself."

Brody returned the embrace. Ryan was no longer the scrawny kid who used to trail after him. His little brother had filled out and grown nearly as tall as himself. Brody felt a pang of guilt for not having kept in better contact with his siblings and for not having helped their older brother Patrick more.

Patrick had stepped in as head of the McClains after their father was killed. Brody had been too traumatized at first even to be aware of how their father's death affected his siblings. Then he'd put all his energy and effort into becoming an officer to carry on in his father's place.

He clapped Ryan on the shoulder as they parted. "You don't look worse for the wear."

Ryan nodded, his chest puffing up slightly. "I do well for myself."

"I know. I've heard. Wheeling and dealing." His mother had told him of his younger brother's passion for accumulating. Brody hoped it wouldn't lead Ryan down a bad path.

He decided when this thing with Kate was over, he'd sit his little brother down and have a long-overdue chat about how money didn't solve problems. Though he doubted Ryan would listen to him. He certainly never had growing up. Why would he start now?

"Wheeling and dealing is what I do best," Ryan said.

Brody couldn't deny that. Ryan had always had an entrepreneurial spirit. Even as a young boy, he'd found ways to make money. Mowing lawns for the neighbors, washing cars for the officers at the station, setting up a lemonade stand. Not just on the sidewalk in front of their house or even the corner of the street. No, Ryan would trudge deep into the park and put his stand near whichever sporting event was taking place. He always came home with his pockets filled with coins. His success probably had more to do with his charm than his lemonade. A good-looking kid, he'd been a big hit, especially with the ladies.

Something that hadn't changed over the years according to his mother. Ryan was the charming one. Always bringing around different girls but never sticking with one for very long.

On the heels of that thought Brody noticed the curious and assessing stare Ryan was giving Kate.

"Who's this lovely lady?" Ryan asked.

"A friend."

Ryan raised a brow. "Mother *will* be pleased. You don't often bring home 'friends.'"

Brody ground his back teeth together. He should have anticipated the assumptions his family would jump to. All he'd been thinking about was keeping Kate safe and getting her somewhere to rest. "It's not like that."

"What a shame," Ryan murmured and moved toward Kate. Brody didn't like the predatory gleam in Ryan's eyes or the grin spreading across the face that had captured and broken many hearts.

"Hello, I'm Ryan McClain." He offered his hand to Kate, his voice charming, smooth.

Brody frowned.

She took his hand, pink brightening her cheeks.

Brody drew back, not liking the way she was reacting and definitely not liking that he even noticed.

"Kate Wheeler," she said, sounding bemused.

"It's a pleasure." Ryan pressed a kiss to the smooth skin on the back of Kate's hand. Her eyes widened and her blush deepened.

An abrupt blast of possessiveness hit Brody like the potent sting of pepper spray. He moved to Kate's side and placed his hand on the small of her back in a purely territorial way. Both Kate and Ryan stared at him in obvious surprise.

"We should go in," Brody said to cover his reaction.

The knowing glint in Ryan's eyes clearly stated he wasn't fooled. Brody chose not to meet Kate's gaze as he ushered her up the front stairs and into the house.

Brody's mind tried to get around what had just happened. He'd never felt anything like this before, not even for Elise. Protectiveness was one thing, but possessiveness? He mentally turned a deaf ear to the warning bells in his head. Now was not the time to try to deal with his foolishness. He needed to keep focused on his purpose for coming to Boston—to protect Kate and find out the truth about why her husband had been killed.

There couldn't be anything more between them than that. He just didn't have it in him to trust anyone that much.

Kate followed Brody as he pushed open the heavy oak front door with the stained-glass windows.

"Mom?" Brody called out.

"Probably in the garden," Ryan stated from behind Kate.

She tried to control the nervous ripple along her limbs at the prospect of meeting Brody's mother. She told herself it was natural to be wary of meeting someone new, but deep down she wanted Mrs. McClain to like her. Though it shouldn't matter. She wasn't Brody's girl.

But Ryan had said Brody didn't often bring home friends. Which meant Brody hadn't introduced his mother to many of the woman he'd dated. Had he brought home the woman who'd hurt him? Jealousy stirred, taking her by surprise. She had no right to feel possessive of him. She held no claim on his affections. No matter what her fanciful heart wished.

She stepped into the foyer and was struck by the bright cheerfulness of the home.

A gleaming hardwood floor stretched beneath her feet and extended into the living room to the left and the formal dining area to the right. A staircase with a polished mahogany banister led to the second floor. She could see the tiled floors and granite counters of the kitchen straight ahead.

The living room was a profusion of color against

dark fabrics and wood-paneled walls. Throw rugs and pillows of assorted shapes looked artlessly placed, yet the whole effect was very welcoming. All sorts of fresh flowers in vases of various styles filled every available space.

Her gaze was drawn to the gilt-framed oil painting above a beautiful mantel and fireplace. The McClain family stared back at her and a sense of awe filled her.

A handsome, uniformed man stood in the background. Dark hair, intense ebony eyes. Brody's father. Kate wondered what type of man he had been. Flanking him on either side were two dark-haired sons. Kate immediately knew which was Brody.

She recognized the earnest smile and wavy hair. She guessed him to be nine. The other boy was taller with a proud tilt to his square jaw and just a hint of a smile as if he hadn't been sure he wanted to relax.

Seated in front of Brody's father was a striking woman with long black hair and crystal-blue eyes. A young girl stood beside her mother, their resemblance uncanny. Both possessed high cheekbones and fair skin. Meghan McClain had also inherited her mother's blue eyes.

A small boy sat on Mrs. McClain's lap. Ryan. Even as a child, his grin was devastating and there was no mistaking the impish light in his dark eyes. Such a lovely family. Sadness touched Kate's heart. This family had lost their father and husband not too many years after this portrait had been done.

"Kate."

She blinked back the tears threatening to escape and turned to find Brody's gaze searching her face. Aware that Ryan stood casually poised by the door frame watching them, she said, "Your home is beautiful."

"I don't live here anymore."

"But it's still your home." Her gaze and her pronouncement included both brothers.

"You hear that, Brody? Sometimes I think you've forgotten." Ryan's softly spoken words held a bit of reprimand but also a dose of hope, as if reminding his older brother that he was still welcome at home might bring him back more often.

A hint of a smile curled the ends of Brody's mouth. "I haven't forgotten."

The men exchanged a silent communication that excluded Kate. Yet, she didn't feel slighted. Instead, a warm glow spread through her. She'd witnessed the bond being strengthened between the two brothers. She'd always wished she'd had siblings.

Then Brody shifted his gaze back to her. Eagerness and tenderness mingled in his expression and melted her heart. "Come out back. I'd like you to meet my mother."

Her mouth went dry. What was she doing? Meeting Brody's mother and being in his childhood home went against the idea of not getting too involved. But she was here and she wouldn't be rude, not after all that Brody had done for her.

She took Brody's offered hand just as the ringing of a phone startled her. Her hand convulsively tightened around Brody's at the jarring noise. Ryan withdrew his small silver cell phone from his pocket and headed up the staircase.

Brody gave her hand a reassuring squeeze. "A little jumpy?"

She smiled sheepishly. "After the day—no, make that the last month, or year, even—I've had, I think I'm allowed."

His dark eyes twinkled. "You are indeed. You're holding up well, Kate. I'm proud of you."

His words made her feel empowered and pleased. She liked that he'd think of her that way. She *was* holding up well, considering someone was trying to kill her and she was growing attached to a man who'd eventually have no more reason to be in her life.

She didn't want to consider why that thought left her more scared than thoughts of her unknown assassins.

FOURTEEN

Brody tugged her hand, urging her to follow him through the kitchen and out the back door into an incredible yard. A brick patio extended from the door about five feet, then a lush lawn, broken only by wood-rimmed flower beds and four distinctive trees ended at the dark-stained fence encircling the whole area.

A woman with a trowel in her gloved hand knelt beside a multi-colored rainbow of perennials. She was dressed in blue denim overalls, a red shirt and green rubber garden shoes. She flipped a long, dark braid over her shoulder as she turned her head at the sound of their approach.

Bright, clear blue eyes widened for a fraction of a second before unabashed joy spread over the older woman's face. Mrs. McClain gave a cry of glee before she scrambled to her feet and hurried to throw herself into Brody's arms.

Kate hung back, feeling uncomfortable watching the affectionate reunion. She'd never had that kind of reaction from her parents. Her father might go as far as to shake her hand and her mother...well, if she were sober she might give her a stiff hug. But certainly not with the kind of happiness Brody was receiving from his mother.

"Let me look at you." Brody's mom held him at arm's length. Though she wasn't as tall as her middle son, her carriage and presence made her a statuesque woman. "I scarcely believed Sean when he called to say you'd been at the station."

Mrs. McClain's gaze captured Kate over Brody's shoulder. Kate straightened under the curiosity and was relieved to see the smile now directed at her was genuine.

Mrs. McClain turned wide eyes to Brody. "Don't be rude, son. Introduce me to your friend."

Brody's neck reddened, but the expression on his face was tender.

Kate swallowed back the choking guilt for using him so ruthlessly.

"Mother, this is Kate Wheeler."

Mrs. McClain peeled off her garden gloves and tossed them onto a wooden bench before holding out her hand. "Hello, Kate."

She took the offered hand, liking the woman's forthright way. "Hello, Mrs. McClain. It's a pleasure to meet you."

The older woman held on to her hand for a moment. Her blue eyes searched Kate's face before she responded. "I'm happy you're here. And please, call me Colleen."

Kate's heart spasmed. It felt good to be wanted. Colleen gave Kate's hand a squeeze, as if she could sense the emotion welling inside her, before letting go.

Colleen slanted Brody a glance. "You're staying for dinner?"

He nodded. "Yes. I was hoping Meggie might have some extra clothes here that Kate could borrow."

Kate inwardly cringed. What kind of impression was she making on Colleen by being so needy?

"Of course she does." Colleen looped her arm through Kate's. "Come with me, dear. We'll get you set up nicely."

Overwhelmed by Colleen's kindness, Kate met Brody's gaze. He smiled reassuringly and urged her on with a tilt of his head. Clutching her purse to her side, she allowed Colleen to lead her back into the house. The feeling of welcome and comfort surrounding her formed a knot in her chest. It wasn't right that she was here, that Brody's family was opening their home to her when she was using Brody so horribly for her own protection.

But what choice did she have?

After Kate and his mom left, Brody sat down in a cushioned patio chair and allowed the quiet of the garden to ease some of the tension from his body. He'd always loved to come out here when life had become too much. The shrink he'd been forced to see after his father's death, and again after Elise, had suggested he find a place where he could think. He'd known his mother came to the garden when she wanted to talk with God. So he'd come back here.

Brody had tried talking to God a few times, but the guilt and anger riding him would always become overwhelming. As he'd grown older, he'd learned how to keep the accusations and the self-recriminations at bay, but a deep emptiness kept him from finding peace.

Still kept him from finding peace.

God wept with you.

Brody scrubbed a hand over his gritty eyes. Kate's assurance, her rock-steady faith, gave him some comfort. And yet the cavernous space inside his chest seemed to expand and press on him, urging him to…to what, he didn't know.

Grace.

The word reverberated around his head and his soul, frustrating him because he didn't get how God's grace applied to his life.

He forced his thoughts to the present situation. They had to find the disk. That was the only way he could guarantee Kate's safety. The only way they could figure out the future.

Tension slammed through him. Did he want a future with Kate?

He stood and restlessly paced the brick patio.

He liked Kate. Liked her humor and her spunk. Enjoyed her company. He was attracted to her as all get out. Warning bells of alarm erupted within him, sending his heart rate through the roof.

He cared for her, that much was true. But he'd been down that road. And until he'd met Kate, he'd never thought he'd go again.

But Kate was not Elise.

The situation was different. *She* was different.

He rubbed a hand through his hair. They had to find

that disk before he could even analyze his feelings. Or, he mentally added with a rueful twist of his lips, overcome the obstacle of his career. Kate had said she couldn't live with the danger his career put him in. But upholding justice was more than a career to him, more than a job. It was his life.

He couldn't see any way around that.

Kate's eyelids fluttered open. Dusk was closing in, making her vision tough to focus in the graying light. She took a moment to absorb the unfamiliar room. The tall dresser to the right of the door, the desk and wooden chair by the window. The shelves filled with dolls collecting dust. The four-poster bed beneath her with its frilly comforter and ruffled pillow shams.

In a rush she remembered. She was in Brody's childhood home, lying on his sister's bed.

When Colleen McClain had brought her upstairs, she'd insisted Kate rest after pulling out some leggings and a cute long tunic blouse from the white dresser drawers. Colleen had clucked over her like a mother hen, much as Myrtle had. It warmed Kate to feel so cared for even as guilt pricked her conscience.

She'd been nothing but a burden to Brody since they'd met. It wasn't fair that she was clinging to him for protection when there was no future for them. No matter how much she'd grown to care for him. She didn't want to hurt him or his family.

She wondered where Brody was now. She sat up and dropped her feet to the ground. A plush rug covering the hardwood floor tickled her uncovered toes. Reaching down, she found her shoes and socks and quickly donned them.

Her gaze stalled on the white princess-style phone on the desk. It was time to take Gordon up on his offer of help and time to shift her reliance off Brody.

She called Gordon's office and was told to try his cellular phone. He picked up on the first ring.

"Kate, where are you?"

"In Boston. At the house of…a friend."

"Did you find the disk?"

"No. But we found out Paul's real name."

"Real name?" Surprised showed in his tone. "Kate, I'm confused. What are you talking about?"

She sighed. "We found out he had connections to organized crime."

There was a moment of silence. "I'm shocked. I had no clue."

"He had us all snowed."

"Have you told the authorities what you've found out?"

"That's why I called. I need your help. The FBI are looking for me. They also think I know where the disk is. But I don't."

"My advice to you, Kate, dear, is to return to Los Angeles as soon as possible. You can sell the Havensport property and put this all behind you."

"But Gordon, I have to find the truth. I have to know what Paul was doing and why he dragged me into this mess. I have to find the disk."

"Sometimes the truth does not set us free, Kate."

Frowning at the ominous message, Kate said, "That's not encouraging."

"Where are you?"

She gave him the address.

"I'll be there as soon as possible," he promised.

She hung up and was gripped with the urge to see Brody. Somehow she was going to have to find a way to explain to Brody why she'd called Gordon and why she couldn't continue to use Brody. She prayed that when the time came, inspiration would hit.

Grabbing her purse from the top of the dresser, she opened the door to the hall. She stepped out of the room and instinctively headed left toward the light traveling up the staircase. A fragment of noise coming from her right caught her attention. She spun around and collided with a rock-hard obstacle.

Hands grabbed her shoulders. Her blood froze. They'd found her.

The thought sent panic roaring through her system like a dam bursting loose. A scream tore from her lungs. Her purse dropped to the ground with a clatter, the contents spilling at her feet. She clawed at the hands holding her.

"Take it easy." A deep masculine voice rasped into her panicked mind. The hands released her abruptly. She staggered back and pressed herself against the wall. The man remained motionless in the shadows.

Pounding feet stormed up the staircase. "Kate?"

She flung herself at Brody as he crested the top stair. His strong arms wrapped around her, secure and comforting. She took deep gulping breaths trying to calm her pulse.

"What's going on?" Colleen McClain pushed past Brody and flicked on the hall light. "Is she all right?"

From behind Brody, Ryan's amused voice cut through the tension charging the air. "I think Patrick gave Kate a good scare."

"Patrick?" Kate lifted her head and stared back at the man standing down the hall.

With the light illuminating him, she saw he was indeed tall, with wide shoulders and long legs. He looked like the professor Brody said he was, not a killer. He wore a brown tweed coat and tan slacks. From behind his wire-rimmed glasses his gaze bored into her with dark intensity.

"Who's she?" Patrick asked.

"Brody's friend," Colleen answered.

Patrick's brows rose as his gaze shifted from Kate to Brody. "Really. How interesting."

Brody tensed and Kate expected him to release her but his arms tightened slightly. Pleasure moved through her and guilt made her want to cry. He was silently claiming her and if he didn't live such a dangerous life she'd rejoice.

She looked at Colleen McClain. How had she survived the life and death of her police officer husband?

Though Kate's father hadn't been a law officer, he'd put his life in danger every time he went on a mission. He'd put his military career ahead of his family. When he'd left, it was as if he'd died, he'd so completely disappeared from their lives. It wasn't until Kate was in her midtwenties that he'd made contact with her again. And Kate's mother hadn't fared well. Still wasn't coping with the loss of her husband, her marriage.

Kate wanted the ideal. A normal husband who

worked nine to five with weekends off, the house with the picket fence, two point five kids and a dog. She wanted normal.

A sick feeling settled in the pit of her stomach. She'd thought she had that with Paul. Everything had seemed to be lining up with her plans. But in the end she did end up like her mother—betrayed, abandoned and alone.

Only the strong arms and big body surrounding her belied that thought. She lifted her gaze up to Brody's handsome face. A face so familiar she doubted she'd ever forget a single detail. The sloping flare of his nose and those ebony eyes so full of life. His lips that could be so tender were now pressed into a grim line as he faced his older brother.

Her heart pounded against her breastbone. Maybe she needed to rethink her idea of normal. The possibilities that thought opened up weakened her knees. She leaned into Brody, distracting him from his brother. Their gazes met and his expression softened. She gave him a shaky smile.

Patrick cleared his throat, drawing their attention. "I didn't mean to scare you."

"It's okay."

"Patrick, this is Kate Wheeler. Kate, my older brother Patrick."

Patrick extended his hand and stepped forward, his loafer-clad foot sending a lipstick tube scuttling across the hall floor.

"Oh, no." She'd forgotten about her spilled purse. After disengaging herself from Brody, Kate bent to retrieve her scattered belongings, aware of three sets of male eyes taking inventory of her cosmetics, flowered wallet and other feminine items.

"Boys, why don't you go ready the dining room for dinner?" Colleen took command of the situation. "Kate and I can take care of this."

"Gladly," Patrick said as he stepped around Kate and stopped beside Brody, clapping him on the back. "Welcome home."

"Thanks," Brody said.

"I want to hear how you met Kate," Ryan piped up.

"Yes, do tell," agreed Patrick.

Kate glanced up and met Brody's wry half smile. "It's complicated," he said.

That was an understatement. Kate grinned back at Brody.

He winked and then led his brothers down the stairs.

"You'll have to excuse my sons' curiosity about you. I can count on one hand the number of girls Brody has brought home since he was old enough to date. He was always so focused on his career. You must be pretty special."

Not special enough for Paul to tell her the truth. Daunted by Colleen's pronouncement and unsure how to respond, Kate reached for her purse.

"Ryan, on the other hand, has been bringing girls home by the dozen since he could talk them into coming with him. But he can't seem to commit to just one." There was amusement and sadness in Colleen's voice.

"And Patrick?" Kate asked.

A pensive expression settled on Colleen's face. Tiny

fine lines bracketed her bright blue eyes. She picked up Kate's flowered wallet, her long elegant fingers toyed with the edge. "Patrick has always been serious, even as a child. After my husband died, a great deal of responsibility was heaped onto Patrick's young shoulders. He hasn't let that go yet. I keep praying the right girl will come along one day and he'll realize it's time to start living his own life."

Kate scooped up a handful of items and stuffed them into the purse as she blinked back the sudden tears. One life cut short and so many other lives affected. Guilt for his father's death clung to Brody, Patrick still carried the weight of family responsibility and Ryan couldn't commit. Kate wondered how the fourth child, Meghan, had fared.

"Here." Colleen handed over the wallet.

"Brody still blames himself for his father's death," Kate said gently.

Colleen's hand shook as Kate relieved her of the wallet. She sat back on her heels, her blue eyes round. "He told you."

Kate nodded. Her pulse picked up speed and the few remaining items at her feet were momentarily forgotten. The enormity of Brody telling her about his father was not lost on Kate. Obviously, he didn't share himself with many people.

"Wow." Tears formed in Colleen's eyes making the blue brighter, more vibrant. "He's not to blame, you know."

"I know. But he can't see that. All he sees is that his choice to get out of the car killed his father."

"No!" Colleen wiped furiously at the tears tumbling down her cheeks. "It was Robert's choice that got him killed. He should have never gone there with his son in the car."

Kate couldn't refute that and her heart twisted with sympathy for Brody's mother.

"I'm sorry. I don't usually go off like that."

Reaching out, Kate touched Colleen's hand. "It's okay." She bit her lip and gathered her courage to ask, "Do you regret marrying a policeman?"

Colleen cocked her head to one side. The speculative and knowing look in her gaze sent heat creeping into Kate's face. "Never. It was who he was." Colleen squeezed Kate's hand. "The only thing you can be sure of in life is love. And when you find love, hold on to it."

Kate took a shuddering breath, wishing she could be alone to analyze and decipher her feelings for Brody. She could no longer deny that her feelings for him ran deep. But she didn't know if she had it in her to love a man with such a risky job. "Thank you."

Colleen's smile was wide. "I think I'll be the one thanking *you* someday."

Afraid Colleen would see the conflict going on inside her, Kate ducked her head and quickly gathered the last of the items and stuffed them into the purse before standing.

"Oh, no," Colleen exclaimed as she stood beside her.

"What?" Kate held up her purse. The hard-sided bottom hung at a crazy angle. She sighed. "When I dropped it, it must have broken. Oh, well." She'd actually be glad to get rid of all reminders of Paul.

"Here, let me see." Colleen took the bag and fiddled with the extending piece. Under her manipulations it slipped back into place with a slight click. "I thought so. I have a purse that has a compartment like this one."

"A compartment?" Kate examined the bottom as her pulse leapt. "How does it work?"

"Press under the edge."

Kate did, and the bottom moved. Why hadn't she ever noticed that? Paul must have known, since he'd given her the thing. Her mind raced to a conclusion that made her tremble with excitement. Could it be? She pushed the stiff plastic piece farther aside and stuck her hand into the dark interior to the bottom of her purse.

Nothing.

Disappointment crashed over her, making tears burn the back of her eyes. Of course, it wouldn't be that easy. She closed her eyes for a second to gather her composure. Deep masculine laughter from downstairs reached her ears. She found comfort in the noise.

"I love the sound of my boys filling the house." Colleen said. "I wish Meggie were home, too." The jingle of a phone sounded from somewhere downstairs. "Better go get that." Colleen moved toward the stairs. "Oops." She bent down and picked up something. Holding out her hand, she said, "Is this yours?"

Kate gaped at the small flat silver disk lying in Colleen's palm. With a hand that shook, she took the disk.

Colleen started moving again. She paused on the top step. "Kate?"

Dumbfounded, Kate lifted her gaze. "I...uh. I'll be right there."

"Okay. Don't be long." Colleen disappeared down the stairs.

Kate's legs felt like rubber. She leaned against the wall.

She had the disk. In her hands was the key to her future. It must have dropped out when the compartment first opened.

"Thank You, Lord," she whispered, grateful that an end was in sight.

They'd hand the disk over to Gabe or the FBI and then it would all be done. The truth would be out and she'd be set free from the prison of not knowing. She'd find the peace she craved.

Brody. She had to tell him she'd found the disk. She pushed away from the wall and raced down the stairs. She skidded to a halt in the foyer. Brody was on the phone.

"Brody," she whispered urgently to get his attention. The news of the disk threatened to burst from her.

He held up a hand and shook his head indicating she needed to wait. He turned his back and spoke low into the phone. Kate frowned, wondering who he was talking to. She moved closer.

"I know my job. I'll bring her in."

Kate drew back her chin. The edge of the disk cut into her palm. She backed up a step as disappointment rolled through her, a deep hurt quick on its heels. Though why she'd care that she was nothing more than a job to Brody, she didn't know. She'd made it clear they had no future together and he'd agreed. It was as simple as that.

She continued to retreat, putting distance between them. Her gaze dropped to the disk in her hand, the light from the chandelier reflected off the silver coating. People were willing to kill for the information on the disk. Willing to kill *her.*

Deciding it would be wise to be forewarned before she handed the disk over to the police, Kate turned, intending to run up the stairs to the den where she'd seen a desktop computer. Instead she found herself once again slamming into Patrick's chest.

She backpedaled and blinked up at him. "Do you always sneak around like that?"

He raised an imperious brow. "Don't you ever look where you're going?"

Without commenting, she slipped the disk into the opening of her purse and made to move around him toward the stairs.

"The dining room is this way," he said, making a sweeping gesture with his arm.

Behind her Brody hung up the phone, effectively cutting off her chance to slip upstairs to view the disk. With a tight smile at Patrick, she marched ahead of the two brothers into the dining room.

"Sit here, dear." Colleen patted a high-backed, dark cherrywood chair.

Brody edged around Kate and pulled out the chair. She took her seat, shaking with guilt for not sharing her find with him. She almost stopped him as he moved to help his mother bring out the food.

Instead, she folded her hands in her lap over her

purse in a protective gesture. For now, the disk lying inside her purse would be her little secret.

She glanced up and caught Brody's gaze. She tried to smile but nausea churned in her stomach.

She hated breaking her promise to Brody.

FIFTEEN

Concern arched through Brody. Kate's complexion had gone pasty and she ate very little as she moved his mother's beef stew around in her bowl. After dodging bullets, running for her life and finding out about her dead husband, he wasn't surprised her scare with Patrick had rattled her.

Just as Gabe's call had rattled Brody. Gabe had said the Feds were checking into Olga and Mrs. Klein. But they'd warned Gabe that they were still seeking Kate. Gabe had rather forcefully suggested Brody bring Kate in so that Brody wouldn't come under any scrutiny for aiding and abetting.

Brody's jaw tightened. He'd told Gabe he'd bring Kate in. But first he had to know who was trying to kill her and make sure they were stopped.

He couldn't live with himself if anything happened to her. He'd promised to help her and he would live up to his promises.

As soon as an opportunity arose to make a polite exit, Kate left the confines of the dining room with the wonderful chatter of Brody's family echoing in her ears. Her heart throbbed with yearning—to belong, to be a part of the McClains. But that possibility didn't exist.

Brody was committed to his job above all else. She wanted a safe and risk-free life. And she was hiding an important piece of evidence from him.

Three outs. Game over. Loser goes to jail.

She didn't want to go to jail. She shuddered at the thought of living day in and day out inside a small concrete cell.

Better jail than death at the hands of the Russian Mafia.

Kate went into the den and sat down in the plush leather office chair. The masculine accents on the desk and gracing the walls led her to believe the room must be used primarily by Patrick.

Colleen had explained that both Ryan and Patrick had apartments but that Patrick spent a great deal of time still at the house. She'd never met a man so controlled and cold. So unlike either of his brothers. Though there was a calculated gleam to Ryan, he oozed of charm, while Brody brimmed with energy and compassion.

A pang of longing plucked at her heart. She'd grown used to relying on Brody's strength. She turned her attention to the computer. When Gordon arrived, he'd know what to do.

The computer took precious moments to boot up. "Come on, come on," she muttered.

As soon as the desktop screen appeared, she deftly slid the disk into the CD-ROM holder.

With a few clicks, the disk downloaded. A security screen box requiring a password popped up. Her mind raced with possible access codes. She typed in the obvious. Paul's name. She tried all three names. Nothing.

She tried the name of the import business Olga talked about. Access denied. She typed in Olga's name. Again denied. Frustrated, she clenched her fist.

"I could use a little help here, Lord," she prayed.

Her hands hovered over the keys. Her mind replayed Gabe's words. The FBI believed she had the information to blow apart a money-laundering scam. Okay, so she did have the disk, but what if she had more? What if…

Her fingers tapped at the keys. She tried her name. Didn't work. She tried variations of her name and Paul's name. She tried the name of her bank. Again access denied.

An idea formed in her mind. She sat straighter, her blood pounded in her ears. Her hands began to shake as she typed in the word *Lillian,* her grandmother's middle name. The word that she used as a password at the bank.

With growing horror she watched the screen shift. Continuing to use the personal numeric codes and passwords that she'd used on her job, she was soon navigating her way through financial spreadsheets, complete with names of businesses, contacts and account numbers. And all of this was being passed through her bank.

She'd never revealed the security codes to Paul, so how had he gotten them? She covered her face with her hands. Had he drugged her? Hypnotized her? Brainwashed her? The depth of the violation sent a shudder racking her body. A panicked flutter hit her stomach, making her ill. Brody would never believe she didn't know about this.

She dropped her fingers back to the keyboard, closing the information and then ejecting the disk. No one knew she had it. Only the bad guys knew what information it contained. She could easily destroy the evidence that implicated her and no one would be the wiser.

She tapped the nails of her right hand on the desk while in her left palm the disk lay ready. All she'd have to do was run her nails over the CD, rendering it useless.

Anyone would believe the scratches happened while bouncing around inside her purse. No one would think she'd done it. Then the Feds wouldn't have anything on her and the bad guys would no longer have a reason to try to kill her. Her pulse picked up speed.

She could walk away scot-free.

She frowned, struggling against what her grandmother had raised her to believe. There was no gray area when it came to right or wrong. God's word was clear. If she truly believed in God and His word, she wouldn't give in to fear and self-protection.

A line of scripture came to her, from Proverbs, she was pretty sure. *The fear of man brings a snare, But he who trusts in the Lord will be exalted.*

If she truly believed, she'd trust Jesus to protect her. He'd sent Brody to protect her, after all.

God had proven Himself worthy of her trust.

She took in a deep calming breath. She wouldn't let her fear of jail lure her into doing something she knew was wrong. She wouldn't deface the disk. She wouldn't destroy Brody's trust.

"Destroying that would solve all your problems, wouldn't it?"

She jerked around to find herself face to face with Brody, who stood in the doorway. The hurt in his dark eyes knocked the breath from her lungs. Slowly, she laid the disk on the desk and backed away. Her soul screamed in despair.

She'd never be able to convince him she wasn't one of the bad guys.

Betrayal pressed in on Brody's chest with crushing intensity. She'd sucked him in, with her pretty face and talk of faith. She'd made him believe in himself, in her. Had made him want to believe in God again. He'd been such a fool. Bile churned in his gut. He clenched his back teeth.

"I know this looks bad, but it's not what you think," Kate said with measured softness.

He arched a brow. "Really. What is it, then?" he ground out. He stalked forward to stand directly in front of her. He swallowed against the tightness in his throat. "You lied to me, Kate. You had the disk all along."

"No. Yes." She shook her head. "I mean…I did have the disk, but I didn't lie to you. I swear." The distress in her eyes seemed so real. "When I dropped my purse in the hall a secret compartment in the bottom opened and the disk came out. Honestly, I didn't know it was there."

"You expect me to believe that?" He curled his lip in a sneer.

But he had. Over and over again.

Every time she'd claimed to be innocent, he'd lapped it up just like a lovesick puppy. He hadn't kept his focus on the job. He hadn't used good judgment. "You used me."

Her blue eyes beseeched him to believe her. "Brody, please. I've never lied to you."

"Save it. I'm not going to believe anything you say." He moved to the desk and picked up the silver disk. Amazing something so little, so ordinary could cause so much chaos.

"What do we do now?"

Kate's voice, so vulnerable and full of anguish, sliced through his chest.

He momentarily closed his eyes against the pain and hardened his heart. He opened his eyes and met her un-flinching gaze. "I do my job."

Her mouth twisted ruefully. "That's what I admire most about you, Brody. Your honor and your integrity."

A single tear crested her long lashes and fell to her cheek, doing more damage to him than a bullet ever could.

Because he loved her.

Even more than his job.

Kate's heart was breaking.

Brody believed she was guilty.

And he didn't even know the worst of it yet. But he would soon and then there'd never be a way to bridge the abyss between them. Though they couldn't have a future together, she couldn't stand the idea he'd go through life believing the worst of her.

She tried to be strong, tried to hold back the tears, but they wouldn't cooperate. With jerky movements, she wiped at the wetness on her cheeks. Taking a deep breath, she silently prayed, *God, what do I do now?*

However futile the effort, she had to try to convince Brody that she hadn't used him. But she didn't know what to say. Every word that popped into her mind seemed contrite and useless.

Suddenly, Ryan appeared in the doorway, his face flushed.

Brody glared at him. "Ryan, we're in the middle of something here."

Ryan stepped inside and pulled the door closed. "There are two Federal Agents downstairs and they want Kate."

The urgency in his voice sent panic ricocheting around her chest. If Brody didn't believe in her, how would she ever convince the FBI she wasn't a party to her husband's dealings?

Brody's silent, grim expression didn't bode well. His eyes drilled her to the floor. She forced herself not to squirm under his scrutiny. She had to trust that God would protect her.

In a swift movement, Brody pulled Kate toward Ryan. Her heart withered in agony in her chest at the cavalier way he was dismissing her.

"Here." Brody shoved the disk at Kate.

Surprised, she reflexively closed her hand around the edge. "What…?"

Brody's voice dropped to a low whisper as he spoke to Ryan. "Do you remember how Meggie used to sneak out of the house?"

Ryan's brows lowered. "Yes."

"Take her out that way," he instructed his brother. Then he turned to Kate.

Her breath hitched at the hurt in his ebony eyes.

"I'll keep the Feds distracted as long as I can." He dug in his pocket for his wallet, pulled out the bills and handed her the cash.

She recoiled in bewilderment. "No."

He opened the door, pushed the money into her hand and then firmly steered her out into the hall. "Go. Just go."

He pivoted and stiffly disappeared down the stairs.

"Come on," Ryan urged.

Why wasn't Brody arresting her?

Too shocked to react, she allowed Ryan to nudge her into Meghan's bedroom and over to the window. He lifted the window sash. "The trellis is sturdy. There's a small drop at the end but you'll do fine. Go through the garden to the back gate. From there head west to the end of the block. You can catch a cab to the train station or the airport." He dug in his pocket and produced a wad of green bills, which he handed to her. "Here, better safe than sorry."

Confused, she shook her head. "Why are you doing this?"

His grim expression matched his brother's. "I trust Brody's judgment. You'd better hurry." He reached for her hand and gave it a quick squeeze. "God go with you, Kate."

Unnerved, she climbed through the window and clung to the trellis. Slowly, she made her way downward, her feet testing each rung as she descended.

The drop to the ground jarred her knees and she stumbled forward before regaining her balance.

With a furtive glance at the house, she hurried toward the back gate and stepped out into the alley that stretched behind the row of houses. She stared down the alleyway to where it ended at a busy street. Cars whizzed past in a blur of color.

Still reeling, Kate tried to make sense of Brody's actions. He'd accused her of lying to him. He clearly believed she was guilty of something, yet he'd let her go. She knew him well enough to know that not turning her in went against everything he was made of.

He was jeopardizing his career for her. Her heart thundered in her chest. Could he care for her, even believing she was guilty? Her mind grappled with that thread of thought. He cared. But did he love her?

And what if he did? Could she allow herself to love a man whose life was constantly in danger?

She tightened her jaw and started forward with purpose. She knew what she had to do.

As Brody came down the stairs, he found Patrick and his mother barring the doorway to the house. Brody hung back for a moment to give Kate a few more seconds and to watch.

Though his older brother was an academic, Patrick cut an intimidating figure when he chose to. His six-two, two-hundred-and-twenty-pound body was an effective blockade and combined with his mother's Irish fire, the Feds didn't stand a chance. His family stood together. He was going to stand by Kate no matter what.

Finally, Brody stepped forward to face the consequences of his folly. "I can take it from here, Patrick. Mom."

"What is going on, Brody? What kind of trouble is Kate in?" demanded Colleen McClain.

"I'll explain later." Brody met Patrick's gaze over his mother's head. "Could you?"

Though Patrick's firm mouth was set in a disapproving line, he nodded. "Of course. Mother, this way." He propelled Colleen away from the door toward the kitchen.

Brody settled himself against the door frame as if he didn't have a care in the world, when inside, his heart ached in a way he'd never experienced before.

He'd known that letting Kate go would cost him his job and his self-respect, he just wasn't prepared for the pain of knowing he'd never see her again. He loathed the thought that she was out there running for her life alone.

But he'd done what he could by giving her time to get away.

Brody hated the way the two Federal Agents looked down their condescending noses at him as if he was some scumbag perp they'd like nothing better than to bust upside the head. Each agent flashed a badge.

"Where is Mrs. Wheeler?" the short agent, Tumbolt, asked.

Brody shrugged off the question. "I don't know. She left."

"She was last seen with you," the tall one, Heinsfled, said.

"Hey, if you want to search the house, feel free. She's not here."

"Where is she?" Heinsfled asked.

He hoped she was safely on her way to the airport. "I don't know. She didn't say."

"You do understand you are obstructing our investigation. As a fellow officer of the law, one would think you'd be more cooperative," Tumbolt said.

Brody thought he might be sick all over the Feds' shiny black shoes.

"Are you looking for me?"

Brody's blood froze at the sound of Kate's voice.

The two agents turned as one and then stepped down the stairs, moving quickly toward Kate. Brody blinked, hoping his mind was playing tricks and that Kate wasn't standing there on his mother's front lawn handing the silver disk to the FBI. He rushed down the stairs and gripped her arm. "What are you doing?"

Her big springtime eyes bored into him with clarity and honesty. "I would rather live wrongly accused than let the man I love sacrifice all that he is for me."

Brody's jaw dropped as her words reverberated through his brain. She was turning herself in because she loved him. His heart squeezed then seemed to expand, filling him with a deep abiding warmth.

Tumbolt stepped forward. "Sheriff McClain, step away from Ms. Wheeler. We are taking her into custody."

Shaken by her admission, he stared at the man, trying to understand what he'd just said. Then Kate's hand covered his on her arm, drawing his attention. Her beautiful face was composed and serene. "It'll be okay," she said as she pried his fingers loose. "God will protect me."

He snapped out of his momentary stupor and scowled. "I'm coming with you."

"That won't be necessary," Heinsfled said as he took Kate's arm and began to lead her away.

Tumbolt stepped in front of Brody as Brody moved to follow. "Sheriff, this is no longer your concern."

Brody fought the urge to plant his fist in the agent's face. The last thing he needed was to be detained for assaulting a fellow officer. He wouldn't be able to help Kate that way. "I'll call your lawyer," he assured Kate.

Her smile was grateful. The agent cuffed her and then helped her into the dark blue sedan parked next to the sidewalk behind Ryan's black car.

Within moments, Kate was gone and Brody felt as if his heart had been ripped from his chest.

She loved him.

Unbelievable.

Kindhearted Kate, with her giving and compassionate nature, loved him.

Moved to the depths of his soul by her selflessness, Brody couldn't deny his feelings for her any longer.

He loved her.

Innocent or guilty.

And he wasn't about to let her throw her life away without a fight.

Lord, You know Kate's heart. I'm asking You for Your help here. If not for me, then for her.

He rushed back inside the house and placed a long-distance call to Gordon Thomas's law office.

On the third ring Gordon's secretary answered. Brody identified himself and asked to speak to the lawyer. He was informed that Mr. Thomas was away from the office but could be reached on his cellular phone.

Within a few moments, Gordon Thomas was on the line. "Sheriff. To what do I owe the honor?"

"Kate Wheeler has been taken into custody in Boston by the FBI. She needs her lawyer."

There was a prolonged silence.

"Did you hear me?" Brody demanded. "Kate needs you."

"Does the FBI have the disk?"

Gordon's calm tone grated on Brody's nerves. What was wrong with the man? Brody frowned. "Yes."

"I'm leaving now," Gordon said abruptly and then hung up.

Brody returned the receiver to its cradle. He should feel better knowing that Kate's lawyer was on his way. But the man still had to fly clear across the country, which would take time. Time that Kate would spend behind bars.

There had to be something he was missing.

Maybe he was looking at this all wrong. Instead of trying to find Petrov's beginnings, he should have been concentrating on Paul's ending. There had to be someone else involved.

Brody would pick apart Paul Wheeler's life. He'd work backwards through Paul's life until he found the connection that would unravel the web of deception surrounding Kate. Because only then would he be able to think about their future together.

His brothers and mother entered the room.

"What now, Brody?" asked Ryan.

Brody didn't have an answer to that.

"Would you please tell me what's going on?" Colleen asked.

Brody headed toward the door. "When I come back I'll tell you everything."

"Where are you going?" Patrick asked.

Brody paused with his hand on the doorknob. "I'm going to find some way to help Kate."

He left the house and hurried through the park back to the station. He blew through the doors and headed straight for Gabe's desk. "I need your help again."

Gabe's eyes narrowed. "What? Someone empty out your pension fund?"

"Worse. The FBI took Kate into custody."

Gabe rolled his eyes. "Back to her, are we?"

Brody didn't have time for his friend's cynicism. "Look. I want to dissect her late husband's life. This time I want to work backwards starting with Paul Wheeler. I want to run background checks on anyone he or Kate had dealings with, starting with their lawyer. I want to tear this identity apart."

"That's a big order." Gabe set his elbows on the desk and steepled his fingers. "You sure she's worth it?"

Gabe's question wasn't surprising. He'd seen what had happened with Elise. But even before that, Gabe had been the perennial bachelor. Always scoffing at others who had found love. Predicting every relationship's demise. And on the occasions when his predictions came true, he gloated, feeling proven right.

"I love her," Brody answered simply, honestly.

Gabe raised a skeptical brow. "It's different this time?"

"Yeah, very different." He was willing to lay down his own life for her.

Gabe groaned. "Save me from romantic fools."

"You going to help me or not?" Brody snapped.

"Yeah, yeah. Grab a seat."

Brody dragged over a chair. For the next hour, he and Gabe surfed through the police network of information. They sifted through Paul Wheeler's life, then shifted their focus to Pete Kinsey. The two identities shared one common thread. Gordon Thomas was the active lawyer for both men. Heart racing with anticipation, Brody had Gabe delve into Petrov Klein's life and the Lanskis' import business.

After digging through layers of misleading and miscellaneous information, Brody found what he was looking for. One of the lawyers acting on behalf of Lanski Imports in a small claims case was none other than Gordon Thomas. The connection was slim, but still there.

If nothing else, it would give the Feds someone else to focus on.

Armed with this information, Brody left the station and took a cab to the new federal courthouse. The Moakley Courthouse located right on Boston Harbor had a stately presence with its redbrick exterior, glass atrium and brass appointments.

At the door, Brody showed his identification and was directed to the fourth floor where two agents, one with dark hair, the other with brown hair, both wearing dark blue suits, approached him. These weren't the same agents who'd taken Kate away. He identified himself.

"I'm Agent Brewster," said the dark-haired man.

"Agent Foster," the brown-haired man said curtly. "Sheriff, what can we do for you?"

"I want to speak with whoever is handling the investigation of Kate Wheeler."

"Right this way." Foster pivoted and led the way down a carpeted hall to a small office with a view of the harbor. Agent Foster preceded Brody into the office. Behind the desk sat a balding man in his sixties who rose as the men filed in. Agent Brewster brought up the rear, shutting the door behind him.

"Sheriff McClain, Special Agent in Charge, Frank Monroe." Foster inclined his head and stepped discreetly back.

Brody held out the file folder with copies of the information Gabe had printed off. "I have information in here that links a lawyer named Gordon Thomas to Paul Wheeler and the Lanskis' import business. I think you should check him out."

Agent Monroe raised a brow. "We know all about Mr. Thomas."

"Then why is he free and Kate Wheeler in custody?" Brody asked sharply.

Agent Monroe shook his head. "We have not secured Kate Wheeler's whereabouts. We were under the impression that she was with you."

Brody blinked. "What? Wait a sec." He fought the

tightening in his chest. "Two agents took her into custody over an hour ago. She's here somewhere."

Monroe exchanged glances with the other two agents. "What kind of game are you trying to play here, Sheriff McClain?"

A very bad feeling gripped Brody. "This is no game. Two agents. Tumbolt and Heinsfled. They have her."

Monroe frowned. "We have no agents by that name in this office. Did they show ID?"

Gritting his teeth, Brody managed to contain his anger at the insinuation that he'd failed to protect Kate. "Yes. They did."

Monroe picked up the phone. "Get me Quantico." A minute later, he hung up the phone. "I'd say we have a problem," Special Agent in Charge Monroe said grimly.

A fist of panic slammed into Brody's midsection, effectively pushing the air from his lungs.

Recovering his breath, his forced his emotions to a far corner. *Stay focused.* He had to save Kate.

And he had a good idea where to start.

SIXTEEN

Kate sat in the backseat of the Feds' sedan, her hands cuffed uncomfortably behind her. She'd done this once before. The night Brody had arrested her in Paul's home. Little did she realized then that she'd fall in love with the sheriff.

Or that she'd cause him so much grief.

The look in his eyes when she'd stepped out from the side of Colleen McClain's home would forever be engraved in her mind. His stunned disbelief had given way to pain. On her behalf. His concern for her moved her deeply and had prompted her to admit why she was turning herself in.

She'd shaken him with her declaration of love. She prayed he didn't think her words were some ploy to garner sympathy from him. She prayed he understood that her feelings were true. And she hoped that someday she'd have a chance to reaffirm her words.

Through the side window she watched the buildings, the neighborhoods, roll by. When the car headed for the on-ramp to the freeway heading north, Kate sat up straighter. "Uh, excuse me. Where are we going?"

When no reply came, she leaned forward. "Hey. Where are you taking me? Why are we leaving Boston?"

The taller agent sitting in the passenger seat glanced over his shoulder. "Headquarters," he said succinctly.

They were driving all the way to Virginia? Kate sat back and settled in, as best she could with her hands cuffed behind her back, for the long drive.

She must have zoned out, because the blast of a horn startled her upright in her seat. Heart pounding in her ears, she blinked at the sight that met her through the window. The Statue of Liberty rose like a beacon from her place on Ellis Island. They were back in New York. Kate craned her neck to read the passing sign. They were on the Staten Island Expressway approaching the Verrazano Narrows toll bridge that would take them into Brooklyn.

"Hey, why are we here?" she demanded.

Silence met her question. A tight ball of apprehension gathered in her chest. She would not be kept in the dark. She kicked the back of the front seat.

The man in the passenger seat whipped around to glare at her. "Be still," he snapped.

"Where are you taking me?" she asked again as droplets of fear began to rain all over her, prickling her skin and raising the hairs at the nape of her neck.

"You'll see." His mouth twisted into a menacing smile. Then to the driver he said something in a foreign language that sounded suspiciously like Russian. The two men laughed at some shared joke.

The muscles in her throat constricted. For a moment, she choked on fear. What had she gotten herself into now? She tried to think clearly. Obviously, she was in the hands of Russian mobsters, on the way to some mob headquarters. How could she escape? She had to keep her mind focused and watch for an opportunity.

But for now, the only thing she could do was pray because whatever path God had set her on, she wanted to face it with the same honor, integrity and bravery that she admired so much in Brody. He'd lost so much, yet he'd persevered. He hadn't let the anger of betrayal turn him into a bitter man. Instead, he'd worked hard to overcome his past and make peace with it.

The car pulled to a stop in front of Lanski's Imports.

Somehow she wasn't totally surprised. Since Paul as Petrov worked for Lanski, it would stand to reason that Mr. Lanski would be involved with the Russian mob.

She was pulled out of the car and led through the warehouse doors. She looked for an opportunity to escape, but being wedged between the two men with each of her elbows firmly within their grasp, she had little hope of getting away. Yet.

She tried to catch the eye of one of the workers but the men working in the warehouse went about their business as if these two thugs strolled in with a hand-cuffed woman every day. Acid churned in her gut.

Instead of being taken up the stairs to Mr. Lanski's office, she was led to a large storage room with a concrete floor and no windows. In the center of the empty room was a single metal chair.

A hot jolt of fear hit her square in the chest. She

backed up as gruesome thoughts of torture assaulted her imagination. The men holding her by the elbows dragged her forward, their fingers digging painfully in to her flesh. Taking quick gasps, she forced herself to hold it together the way Brody would.

"Sit," ordered the man who'd driven the car. He planted his meaty hand in the middle of her back and shoved her forward.

Kate stumbled, but quickly regained her balance. Figuring it safer to comply than to resist any more until she had a better idea what they intended to do with her, she sat on the cold chair, her knees knocking together.

The men left, shutting the heavy metal door behind them. The ominous click of the lock sliding into place sent a chill rippling over her flesh. She tried to take deep calming breaths, but the musty stale air made her gag. What did they use this room for? Just to hold people against their will? How often did they do that? What were they going to do with her?

After a few minutes she rose from the chair. Sitting like the proverbial duck wasn't helping her to stay calm. She had to find a way out. She looked around. Knowing it was futile, she strode to the door, turned her back and tried the knob. No miracles there.

With the heel of her foot she kicked the door. The metallic echo rang inside her chest, emphasizing the emptiness in her heart. She ached deep inside for Brody, longed for his steady presence. His protection. Did he know she wasn't with the real FBI? Tension tightened the muscles in her neck and shoulders. Her head throbbed.

So many questions still unanswered. So much danger threatening her life.

Suddenly tired of all the intrigue, she sat back in the chair, closed her eyes and prayed. Prayed for rescue, prayed for Brody and prayed to understand why all this was happening to her.

Brody had once said she'd learn to live with the unknown, the questions. As he had. Focus on the needs of the day, he'd also said. An overwhelming desperation clawed at her throat, choking her. How could she do that when she had no control over her present situation?

But wasn't that the crux of her faith? She had no control. God was in control. So instead of asking why, she needed to focus on God's goodness. His faithfulness. And if she died today, she'd be going to Heaven and the answers to all her questions wouldn't matter.

Softly, she began to sing every song of praise she could remember.

What seemed like hours later, the lock on the door rattled and the door swung open. Bracing herself, Kate straightened. The two fake Federal agents walked in, followed by Mr. Lanski and the two men who'd taken her from Myrtle's deck.

Then another man walked in, and Kate gasped with stunned relief. His dark hair, salted with some gray, was styled back away from his lined, aristocratic face. He stared down his patrician nose at her.

"Gordon? What… How did you get here?"

Gordon Thomas tsked as he moved to stand over Kate. "Ah, my dear. This breaks my heart."

With a quick flick of his wrist he addressed the others in the room in fluent Russian. Kate's relief evaporated into shocked disbelief. She couldn't have felt more betrayed. She'd always assumed he was of Latin descent with his dark hair, dark eyes and olive complexion.

One of the thugs stepped forward and uncuffed her hands. She rubbed at the red welts forming on her wrists and rolled the pain from her shoulders.

She stared at Gordon. He was tall, reed-thin and immaculately dressed in a dark suit that screamed designer label. A look more appropriate for a Beverly Hills lawyer than a Russian mobster. Or so she thought.

She remembered what Brody had said about the *Organizatsiya* being well-educated. Obviously, they'd recruited law-school grads into their fold.

"I never meant for you to end up here, Kate. I'd hoped you would find the disk and relinquish it without any trouble. But alas. You were so determined to discover the truth. I did warn you that the truth wouldn't always set you free."

"I don't understand. Why did you ruin my life?"

"Oh, now. Don't think it was personal. You were a convenient way for us to gain access to the bank. You and your mother were so needy. It was really an innovative plan. We waited for you to grow up and I very carefully steered you toward banking. You had such potential. We knew you'd do well at the bank. You exceeded our expectations. Vice President of Operations. Very nice." He smiled in the fatherly way that had brought her such comfort over the years. Bile rose in her throat.

"It was such an easy thing to plant a camera in your home office to obtain your passwords which gained us access to the bank." He shook his head, his expression rueful. "Only, poor Petrov fell in love."

For a second, old dreams stirred, but were instantly obliterated by reality. Her stomach clenched. "With Olga."

Gordon nodded. "True. And he could have had her if he'd just stayed with the program for a bit longer."

Kate hated being referred to as the program, as if her life meant nothing more than a means to their end. They'd orchestrated her marriage and her career. And she'd danced merrily to their tune like a puppet on a string. "Why did you kill him?"

"The disk. We found out he'd been compiling information and recording it all. He'd said he wanted out and the disk was insurance. Ha! No one threatens us and gets away with it."

"Who is us? You and Lanski?" Her gaze swept over the other men in the room. The thugs stared at her dispassionately and Mr. Lanski's scowl deepened. "Are you two the heads of the Russian Mob?"

He tsked again. "Really, Kate. You ask too many questions."

"You're going to kill me anyway, right? So why not tell me everything?"

He sighed. "Come." He held out his hand. "I'd like to show you something."

She stared at his hand, hating the sense of doom seeping through her. After all this, she was going to die. But at least now she had closure where Paul was concerned. And she'd known Brody. Her heart squeezed with sadness and regret that they'd never have a life together.

She allowed Gordon to help her to her feet. He tucked her hand into his elbow and escorted her out of the small room ahead of the other men whose disdain she felt like a thousand pinpricks.

Gordon stopped as Mr. Lanski stepped close and spoke harshly in his mother tongue. The two men argued for a moment before Mr. Lanski waved a hand of dismissal and walked away.

Gordon continued on up the stairs to the office where she and Brody had first met Mr. Lanski. He shut the door behind them. He pulled her over to the computer where the disk had been loaded. She wondered if she should tell him she'd already seen the contents but decided to remain silent. If by some miracle she got away, anything he said might prove useful.

"See, here," Gordon said, "Our business flourishes."

"Business," she scoffed. "Money laundering, you mean."

He frowned. "No need to be rude, Kate."

She rolled her eyes. She had every right to be rude.

"We have many legitimate businesses." He went on to explain the workings of their operation.

Kate listened with growing astonishment. The scope and ingenuity of the operation must have taken years to build. Assets from several legitimate companies were being used to fund several more illegal operations ranging from selling drugs to smuggling diamonds.

Gordon went on to explain how Petrov's parents were immigrants who owed their allegiance to the

people who supplied them with a home in America.
Petrov had done well in his American school and had
been singled out and groomed to infiltrate American
life.

Not to spy for the motherland, but to work for the *Organizatsiya*. When the time came for Petrov to become
useful, Gordon had help to set him up as Pete Kinsey
on the East Coast and Paul Wheeler on the west.

Sickened by the scope and enormity of the operation,
she stared at the man she'd thought of as family. "I
trusted you."

Sudden shouts from outside the office spurred
Gordon to action. He pushed Kate aside and ejected the
disk. Shots rang out and Kate's blood froze.

Then the door burst open. Brody charged in, weapon
drawn. A half dozen more gun-toting men in dark vests
with FBI in bold yellow print across their chests piled in.

Someone shouted, "Don't move!"

Kate tore her relieved gaze from Brody and realized
instantly what Gordon was attempting to do as he seized
the ejected CD.

"No," she shouted and flung herself at him. She
heard Brody yell, "Don't shoot!"

She tried to wrestle the disk out of Gordon's grasp.

Too late. His manicured nails dug rivets into the silver
coating of the disk as they toppled sideways to the ground.

Then there were hands dragging her up and twisting
her arms behind her. She cried out as pain from her
already sore shoulders gripped her. Panicked, she
sought Brody through the sea of Federal agents.

But to her dismay, he was gone.

* * *

"No, you don't." Brody captured Mr. Lanski by the scruff of his neck. He'd seen the man flee the scene in the commotion created by Kate tackling Gordon.

The owner of Lanski's Imports struggled to get away but Brody planted his knee into the older man's kidney. Effectively subdued, Lanski went down to his knees with an oath. Brody cuffed him and pulled him to his feet.

Dragging the heavy Russian back and then handing him over to a Federal agent, Brody assessed the situation and realized that while he was going after Lanski, Kate and Gordon Thomas had been taken into custody and led away.

He raced out of the building in time to see the car they'd said she was in drive away. He stood in the middle of the chaos in the street created by the raid and tried to get himself back under control.

Boy, the way Kate had dived at the man had nearly given Brody a heart attack. For a split second he'd feared the Feds would shoot and ask questions later. The thought of losing her again filled him with dread. And realization.

Deep in his heart he knew she wasn't guilty no matter how bad it might still look even after she'd tried to keep Gordon Thomas from tampering with the disk. Brody'd move heaven and earth to prove her innocence.

Man, she was something. Pride lifted his heart. She still had that spunk he admired. And she was so brave. He loved her for so many reasons.

Thank You, Lord.

Now, he only hoped she'd give him another chance. If giving up being a law officer was the only way she'd have him, then he'd gladly turn over his badge and his weapon.

The trip to the Federal building went by in a blur of tears. She didn't know what to think about Brody's disappearing act. Had he thought she'd been with Gordon by choice? Her heart twisted in her chest.

She was ushered to a small, two-way mirrored room where two agents questioned her endlessly about Gordon, Paul and the disk. She told them everything she could remember. They took notes and seemed pleased with the information she had.

Now, alone, she shifted uncomfortably in the hard metal chair and tried to still the shaking of her hands, but the effort took too much energy. The tomblike quiet in the cold, sterile room stretched her nerves until she thought she'd scream. She'd been left alone in the room with the large mirror for—she glanced at her watch— forty minutes.

The rattle of the doorknob being unlocked sent a shiver of apprehension galloping down her spine. The door swung open and Brody walked in. Her heart leapt, then plummeted at the hooded expression in his eyes. She shifted her gaze away. She didn't want to face his accusations again. She'd break down for sure.

The scraping of the metal legs of a chair brought her chin up.

Brody sat down across from her. "The disk was ruined. The information irretrievable," he said matter-of-factly.

"I tried to stop him." She rubbed her temples. "He killed Paul. He tried to kill me… I trusted him."

Brody's gaze narrowed slightly. "Why did you trust him?"

In her mind, she went back to the day she'd found Paul bleeding to death on the floor of his living room. "Paul said Gordon's name right before he died. I thought Paul had wanted him, was telling me to trust Gordon." Placing her hands flat on the table, she sat up straight as realization hit. "But Paul was trying to warn me."

Brody's expression softened and he reached out to take one of her hands. A tender melting happened somehow in the vicinity of her heart.

"Maybe, maybe not," he said. "He may not have known who was behind his attack. We'll never know."

The pressure of his palm gave her comfort and made her sad all at once. She wanted to cling to him, to confirm her love for him was real. Instead she slipped her hand away. She couldn't take any more hurt and rejection. "Why are you here?"

"You're free, Kate. Thomas confirmed you weren't involved and he's confessed to ordering the hit on Paul and the attempts on your life, but he won't say anything else."

Relief swept through her.

"Even after being offered immunity for murder, he won't roll on his comrades. More afraid of them than prison. Without the solid evidence of the disk, there's no way to charge him with anything more. The information you gave will be helpful in the Feds' investigation into the *Organizatsiya*. Lanski was also brought into custody and will be charged with kidnapping. By all accounts, the import business is legit."

The news that she was exonerated from any wrongdoing was welcome and needed. She should feel vindicated. She wasn't the bad person Brody believed her to be. But as she stared at his ruggedly handsome face, emptiness filled her. She didn't know what Brody felt and without the man she loved in her life, her future seemed pretty desolate.

She fought against the stinging in her eyes. She'd thought peace would come with the truth about Paul, but it hadn't. Closure yes, but not peace. She didn't understand. What was she missing? "But why are *you* here?"

His mouth twisted with humble tenderness. "Because I'm an idiot and I want to beg for your forgiveness."

Her mouth went dry. The first quickening of hope tightened her chest. Could it be true?

Once again he took her hand, turning it palm up and curling his fingers over hers. The gesture, at once possessive and tender, made tears burn the back of her eyelids. "I should have trusted you."

"I understand why you didn't," she said softly.

He shook his head. "I should have believed in what I felt for you."

She swallowed hard, barely daring to let the hope rise any further. "What…what do you feel?"

He leaned forward, crowding away the air between them. Her heart stalled as she looked into his eyes and saw the answer to her question. Barely able to breathe, she waited for the words.

"I love you, Kate. Will you give me another chance? A chance to love you?"

Everything inside her wanted to scream "Yes!" But how could she? Just because they loved each other didn't change the fact that he was a sheriff, risking his life every day, and when push came to shove, she couldn't live like that.

She thought about her parents, about how her father risked his life every time he went on a mission. She thought about how the worry slowly destroyed her mother until finally when her father left, her mother sank into despair and a bottle. She closed her eyes against the pain of having to deny Brody's love. "I'm not brave enough to live that life."

The metal clunk of something hitting the table caused her to open her eyes. In front of her lay his badge and his black, ominous-looking gun. Knowing instantly the significance of his gesture, her gaze jumped to his. "No. I can't ask you to do that. I *won't* ask that of you." She pushed the items toward him. "This is who you are."

Brody's hands cupped her face. "Look at me," he demanded.

She made a noise of distress and shook her head. It hurt her to think he'd be so selfless for her. Especially after realizing how ruthlessly she'd been used.

"Kate, listen to me."

The compelling tone in his voice forced her gaze to lock with his. His earnest and loving expression scored her clean through.

"You are the most courageous woman I've ever

known. You can handle anything. I'm not going to lie to you. Being a law officer is risky, but so are other professions. So is crossing the street or driving a car. You can't live your life in fear. You told me God would protect you. Then trust that He'll protect us both."

His words were an echo of the thoughts she'd had earlier. Anticipation and joy fluttered like the gentle wings of a butterfly, raising her hope till she thought she might float. "Do you trust him?"

A thoughtful gleam entered his gaze. "I don't get what purpose my father's death served or the purpose in my being shot. Pastor Sims talked about God's grace, God's undeserved favor. I'm struggling to get my mind around that. Around how in my weakness His strength is perfected." Slowly, he nodded his head. "But yes, I do trust. Trust that He brought us together. Trust that He'll watch over us. And in time I hope I'll understand this whole grace thing."

His words gladdened her heart and filled her with satisfaction. He was on his way to reconciling his relationship with God. Something good had come out of her ordeal. Could something else good come from such a mess?

Something clicked inside Kate, shifted into focus. If he could reconcile with God, could she reconcile herself to a life of risk?

Brody was right that there were risks in any profession, in any lifestyle. Going the safe route hadn't given her what she'd wanted.

She really needed to reassess what she wanted out of life. Was safe and secure really what she longed for? Would those two elusive concepts satisfy the hunger in her heart?

She drank in Brody's face, memorizing every line, every angle. Deep in her heart, she knew this time around she would chose love and walk in faith that God would continue to be her shield.

"Kate, I need you."

Overwhelmed with love for this man, she leaned forward until their lips were nearly touching. Gazing into his eyes, she let her heart shine. "I prayed for peace and God sent me you."

A smile lit up Brody's eyes. "Will you marry me, Kate? Let me stand watch over you for the rest of your life?"

Joy, pure and good burst from her heart, filling her soul. She touched his cheek, the soft pads of her fingers rubbing against the stubble darkening his jawbone. "Yes. Oh, yes."

With a growl of approval, Brody captured her lips.

Kate reveled in the love and passion igniting between them. No matter how risky life as a sheriff's wife would be, she was confident that the peace and security that could only come from God would sustain her through the years at Brody's side.

This time around, she would be certain to hold on to love.

Forever.

Dear Reader,

Thank you for taking this journey with Kate and Brody as they sifted through the layers of deception to find the truth, and in the process found love.

So often we have to sift through the layers of deception that the world heaps on us to get to the truth of God's love. And in doing so, we bare many scars. My prayer for you is that you'll let God heal your wounds and hurts as only He can. It's hard work figuring out what to believe when the world entices us with money, power and pleasure, but remember always that your Heavenly Father loves you and will always embrace you as you turn to Him.

May God bless you,

QUESTIONS FOR DISCUSSION

1. Out of all the books you could have chosen, why did you choose *Double Deception?* Was it the cover? The back blurb? The author?

2. Kate was stunned when she learned her husband had a secret life. Have you ever been surprised by revelations from loved ones? How did you handle the revelations? Did you pray about them? Why or why not?

3. If you were in Kate's shoes, would you have sought the truth? Would you have gone about it differently? Or would you have charged ahead as Kate did?

4. Sacrifice was an important part of this story. Have you ever had to sacrifice something important to you? How did you feel about it?

5. Brody returns to the faith he'd lost after his father's death. Have you lost someone and questioned or lost your faith? What brought you back to God?

6. Did the villain surprise you? Were there hints that you can pinpoint, or was it a complete surprise?

7. Kate thought she would find peace from knowing the truth, but where does real peace come from? Does living a safe and stable life ensure safety and stability?

8. Brody challenged Kate not to live in fear. Is there something you are living in fear of? Over and over again God's word tells us to fear not. Confess your fear to God and ask for His peace. Read Psalms 56:3.

9. Was this the first book you've read by this author? Would you read more from her? Why or why not?

10. What are your most vivid memories for this book? What lessons about life, love and faith did you learn from this story?

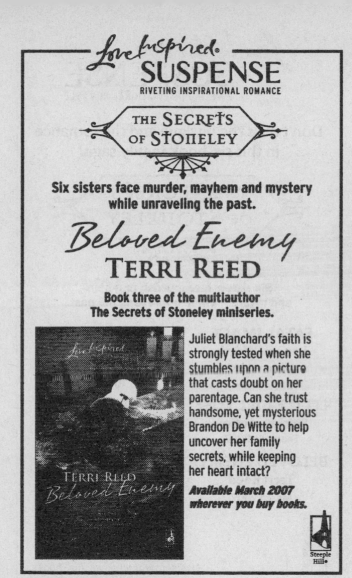

RIVETING INSPIRATIONAL ROMANCE

Don't miss the intrigue and the romance
in this six-book family saga.

Six sisters face murder, mayhem
and mystery while unraveling the past.

FATAL IMAGE
Lenora Worth
January 2007

**THE SOUND
OF SECRETS**
Irene Brand
April 2007

LITTLE GIRL LOST
Shirlee McCoy
February 2007

DEADLY PAYOFF
Valerie Hansen
May 2007

BELOVED ENEMY
Terri Reed
March 2007

**WHERE THE
TRUTH LIES**
Lynn Bulock
June 2007

Steeple
Hill®

Available wherever you buy books.

REQUEST YOUR FREE BOOKS!

2 FREE INSPIRATIONAL NOVELS PLUS 2 FREE MYSTERY GIFTS

YES! Please send me 2 FREE Love Inspired® novels and my 2 FREE mystery gifts. After receiving them, if I don't wish to receive any more books, I can return the shipping statement marked "cancel." If I don't cancel, I will receive 4 brand-new novels every month and be billed just $3.99 per book in the U.S., or $4.74 per book in Canada, plus 25¢ shipping and handling per book and applicable taxes, if any*. That's a savings of 20% off the cover price! I understand that accepting the 2 free books and gifts places me under no obligation to buy anything. I can always return a shipment and cancel at any time. Even if I never buy another book from Steeple Hill, the two free books and gifts are mine to keep forever.

113 IDN EF26   313 IDN EF27

Name	(PLEASE PRINT)
Address	Apt. #
City	State/Prov.	Zip/Postal Code

Signature (if under 18, a parent or guardian must sign)

Order online at www.LoveInspiredBooks.com

Or mail to Steeple Hill Reader Service™:

IN U.S.A.: P.O. Box 1867, Buffalo, NY 14240-1867
IN CANADA: P.O. Box 609, Fort Erie, Ontario L2A 5X3

Not valid to current Love Inspired subscribers.

Want to try two free books from another series?
Call 1-800-873-8635 or visit www.morefreebooks.com

* Terms and prices subject to change without notice. NY residents add applicable sales tax. Canadian residents will be charged applicable provincial taxes and GST. This offer is limited to one order per household. All orders subject to approval. Credit or debit balances in a customer's account(s) may be offset by any other outstanding balance owed by or to the customer. Please allow 4 to 6 weeks for delivery.

Your Privacy: Steeple Hill is committed to protecting your privacy. Our Privacy Policy is available online at www.eHarlequin.com or upon request from the Reader Service. From time to time we make our lists of customers available to reputable firms who may have a product or service of interest to you. If you would prefer we not share your name and address, please check here. ☐

LIREG07

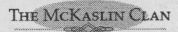

Love Inspired
SUSPENSE

TITLES AVAILABLE NEXT MONTH

Don't miss these four stories in March

SO DARK THE NIGHT by Margaret Daley

On a tragic night, photographer Emma St. James
lost her vision and her memory of her brother's murder.
She was alone on the run from the killers, until Reverend
Colin Fitzpatrick reached out with a touch she couldn't
see....

BELOVED ENEMY by Terri Reed
The Secrets of Stoneley

Juliet Blanchard stumbled upon a picture that cast doubt on
her parentage. With the world crumbling around her, could
she trust handsome newcomer Brandon DeWitte to help her
find the truth without breaking her heart?

SHADOWS OF TRUTH by Sharon Mignerey

Only one thing could bring DEA agent Micah McLeod back to
Carbondale, Colorado: Rachel Neesham was in danger. He'd
vowed to keep her and her two children safe at any cost.
Would Rachel let him? Her life depended on it.

PURSUIT OF JUSTICE by Pamela Tracy

While helping the police bust a drug ring, Rosa Cagnalia
found herself framed for murder. Officer Samuel Packard
suspected that Rosa might be innocent. Now if only he could
get his beautiful suspect to cooperate...

LISCNM0207